W9-BNF-579

Random Acts of
Kittens

YAMILE SAIED MÉNDEZ

Scholastic Inc.

If you purchased this book without a cover, you should be aware that this book is stolen property. It was reported as "unsold and destroyed" to the publisher, and neither the author nor the publisher has received any payment for this "stripped book."

Copyright © 2020 by Yamile Saied Méndez

All rights reserved. Published by Scholastic Inc., *Publishers since 1920.* SCHOLASTIC and associated logos are trademarks and/or registered trademarks of Scholastic Inc.

The publisher does not have any control over and does not assume any responsibility for author or third-party websites or their content.

No part of this publication may be reproduced, stored in a retrieval system, or transmitted in any form or by any means, electronic, mechanical, photocopying, recording, or otherwise, without written permission of the publisher. For information regarding permission, write to Scholastic Inc., Attention: Permissions Department, 557 Broadway, New York, NY 10012.

This book is a work of fiction. Names, characters, places, and incidents are either the product of the author's imagination or are used fictitiously, and any resemblance to actual persons, living or dead, business establishments, events, or locales is entirely coincidental.

ISBN 978-1-338-57492-0

10 9 8 7 6 5 4 3 2 1   20 21 22 23 24

Printed in the U.S.A.   40
First printing 2020

Book design by Jennifer Rinaldi

To Valentino, my real-life Babycat,
Areli, my entrepreneur supreme and
ultimate muse, and mi madrina,
Cristina Silverio Saied,
por todo tu amor.

Chapter 1
Not My Fault

It was all the cat's fault.

In my defense, I only fed it once. Really, how could I have resisted that sweet face? Yesterday when I saw it sitting on the snow-covered picnic table in my backyard, I snuck out of the house and placed a can of organic tuna nearby. I should have known that small decision would wreck my life. Hadn't I learned time after time that no good deed goes unpunished?

Twenty-four hours after my spur-of-the-moment kindness, I heard the telltale sounds of something hungry rummaging in the garbage, apparently looking for more free food. If she heard the noise, Mami would send me out to check. Did she even care that I had things to do or that I was sick with a virus? I didn't dare ask aloud in case the answer hurt more than swallowing rice pudding did.

Just when I thought Mami hadn't heard anything, she muted the cheery Puerto Rican Christmas music on her phone and asked, "What's making that escándalo outside?"

I kept typing at the computer, pretending I couldn't hear the racket, as she'd called it.

"Shhh, Natalia, listen," she whispered, and put the pudgy plastic succulent leaf down on the table. She was making flower arrangements for one of her commissions.

My fingers hovered over the keyboard. The sound of a can clanking on the driveway echoed all the way into the kitchen.

Silly cat. I told it to keep the secret between us. If my mom found out I'd been feeding a stray, she'd ground me for the rest of winter break. Today was only the first day, and as soon as I shook off this bug, I intended to have the most unforgettable staycation ever.

Mami narrowed her eyes and shook her head, as if she

could imagine nothing good happening outside. "Go and make sure the garbage bins are lidded, and while you're at it, take them to the curb. Tomorrow's garbage day."

Although I knew this was coming, I still groaned. "Why is the garbage my job?"

But now *she* was the one pretending to have selective hearing. "I don't want our leftovers attracting sabandijas," she said. "Poor little chickens; they never hurt a soul. They were the happiest creatures ever."

Happy creatures? I almost laughed. Give me a break. Mrs. Lind's rooster would crow its heart out at dark o'clock every morning (and, I swear, even earlier on weekends and holidays). This week I'd slept in for the first time in ages. I was *grateful* the raccoon, or whatever it was, had eaten the chickens.

A terrible possibility flashed in my mind—had the cat eaten the chickens?

No way. The cat I'd fed was too small. It didn't even have a tail, just a fluff. But what if the cat had really been *that* hungry? I knew nothing about cats. I'd have to ask my best friend, Reuben, if it was possible for such a small animal to have that big of an appetite.

I only had time to type the question when Mami said, "Natalia . . ."

"What, Mami?" I rolled my eyes. "I'm talking with Reuben!"

Reuben was also home sick with the same virus. I told him a million times not to drink from my water bottle, but did he ever listen?

When she didn't reply, I swiveled in the computer chair to look at her.

"You're always talking with Reuben. Since you're on that computer all day, you could spend a little minute to send your father a note." She smiled tightly and bobbed her head from side to side.

And this woman wondered who I got the attitude from.

I swiveled the chair back to break the eye contact, but I could still see her reflection on the screen and the smirk on her face. Writing to my dad was a topic I didn't want to discuss right now. Or ever.

"Why are you asking *me* to do it?" I tried to change the subject.

"Because I did it last time and I had to clean up the mess you left. You always leave the lids on the ground."

"I never!" I said . . . even though I *might* have left them on the ground last time. But what was I supposed to do? The bin had been full. "Can't you ask Beli?" I forced a cough and grabbed at my throat for emphasis.

Mami laughed. "Seriously?"

Of course she would never ask my grandma. Beli was a guest, and a reluctant one to boot. She loved us, but she was used to the year-round summer weather in Puerto Rico and hated the cold. She was now in her room, the heater blasting as she watched TV. She wouldn't leave the house unless it was absolutely necessary—or if my sister, Julieta, invited her to go shopping or something.

"What about Julieta, your *favorite*?" As soon as the word was out of my mouth, I wanted to bite my tongue. Telling the truth always got me in trouble.

Mami didn't answer. Of course she wouldn't send Juli to

do anything as undignified as checking on raccoons in the garbage. Julieta always did everything perfectly right, like writing to my dad every week without being asked, plus keeping up with her own dad. She called my dad Papi and hers Dad, and they both adored her. She was everyone's favorite.

I stomped to the door and made a show of putting my puffy red jacket on.

"Gracias, y por favor stop it with that *favorite* business," Mami said, looking smug. "Your sister has been an angel lately. You could learn from her that when you spread kindness, you attract good things in your life."

Julieta wasn't an angel, not to me at least, and seriously, my previous experience proved that kindness didn't always bring good things. I'd fed the cat and now it was practically haunting me.

I made a dramatic exit through the kitchen door that led to the carport, flipping my hair out of my face. Right next to the door was a photo of Papi in his fancy army uniform. Mami had put photos of him all over the house. This one sat on the wall shelf as if he were one of those peeping holiday elves.

The door slammed behind me in the wind, and I heard the photo frame fall. I cringed. Oops. Mami would think I'd thrown the door shut on purpose.

She didn't understand. It's not like I could spread kindness like honey butter on a warm dinner roll. When I'd been nice in the past, people like Meera Rogers had thought I was dumb and taken advantage of me. Never again!

Now, I was pretty sure that as—and I quote Mrs. Snow, the principal—"the most controversial student in Andromeda Elementary," *kind* wasn't the first word that popped into people's minds when they thought of me.

If Papi were here, he wouldn't send me out, or he'd at least come to check on the noise with me. He'd make it into an adventure. Although he loved Juli, he didn't really play favorites, but a part of me liked to think I was his. Now he'd been gone for months, and who knew when he'd be back?

I told myself not to think about it too much and walked toward the bins.

"Gato!" I called in a whisper-shout.

The cat didn't answer, but I saw little paw prints marking the pristine snow. I followed them all the way to the bins lined up by the wall. I glanced up across the street. The Rogerses' house was lit up and decorated for the season, unlike ours. Mami had said this Christmas would be like any other, but the truth was that without Papi nothing was the same. We hadn't even put up a tree.

The Rogerses always had a lot of company over. I recognized their grandparents' car parked at their curb. At least there was no sign of my ex–best friend, Meera. Seeing her every day at school was bad enough. Crossing paths with her in the neighborhood and witnessing her perfect family was the worst.

More crumpling sounds called me to the task at hand.

When I looked behind the bin and yelled, "Fuah!" all I saw was the same scared, small, hungry cat I'd fed yesterday.

It stood frozen, an old slice of pepperoni pizza in its mouth. In the almost darkness, the cat looked black, but yesterday I'd been fascinated with the different colors of its fur—white tummy and feet, red on one side of its face, and black on the other.

"Whew!" I exclaimed. "You're lucky *I* found you! Better be careful! My mom will call animal control if she sees you."

The cat flattened its ears against its head.

Raising my hand, I quickly said, "I come in peace."

Poor cat just stared at me, breathing fast. It didn't have a collar, but it wasn't a pest, a sabandija. It hadn't jumped at me to claw off my face yet. When I stretched out my hand to pet the gatito, it sniffed at me and took a step in my direction. Right then, a neighborhood dog suddenly barked, and the cat darted away straight to our storage shed, where Mami kept old flower arrangement materials and other craft things. She hardly ever went in there in the winter, so it was the secret hiding place for all my forbidden slime supplies.

Yesterday after I fed the cat, I'd gone in there to play with my favorite slime recipes. I'd saved a few tubs from the big purge. It had taken a while for Pink Rose, Slime Supreme's bestselling scent, to soften in my hands, but the work kneading it had been worth it. Playing with slime always soothed me.

Now I couldn't remember if I'd closed the door tightly when I left the shed.

Before I checked to make sure the cat didn't get into any of Mami's things, I dragged the bins to the curb, huffing and puffing with the effort.

While I was fighting with the wind for the lid to stay put on top, Meera Rogers walked out of her house with her dog, Captain America.

I didn't want her to see me, so I stood still, hoping to blend into the shadows. Nothing escaped Cap's attention, though, and he saw me, of course. He barked, all friendly, saying hi. He didn't understand Meera and I weren't friends anymore. But when I looked over, I caught Meera's eye by accident.

Hurriedly, I smashed the garbage bags with the lid and

ran inside my house. I'd have to wait to go check on the cat. I turned to lock the door and almost bumped into Beli.

"What were you doing out in the cold so long, mi amor?" she asked. "Your sore throat won't ever go away if you don't take care of yourself."

"Mami sent me to take the trash out." I tried not to whine.

"In this cold?"

I nodded while holding a hand to my throat and sending Mami a look that meant *See?* which she ignored.

Beli shook her head and clicked her tongue. "You must stay nice and warm if you want to get better! Yesterday you were in that shed for hours! It must be full of mice in there," she mumbled.

Mice! I shivered, and she handed me the steaming cup of hot chocolate she held in her hand as if she'd been just waiting for me. Warmth spread all over me with her lovely gesture.

"Gracias, Beli!" I took a sip and scalded my tongue. "Ay! It's hot!"

"Sorry!" She winced. "You know I'm not the best judge of temperature in this cold. Brrrr, I can't wait to go back to the island."

From the kitchen table, where she was putting away the flower cuttings, jars, decorative sand, and ribbons scattered all around, Mami sighed. "Ay, Mami!" she said to Beli, whining in the same voice I used, the one she always complained about. "At least pretend you're happy to be here. Mako has you all year long, and the girls and I need you too."

Mako was my uncle, Tío Manuel Joaquín, and Beli lived with him and his family in the most gorgeous beach house in Puerto Rico.

"Gina, bebé," Beli said as she went over to Mami and kissed the top of her head. "You'll always be my favorite girl. You know that, cierto?"

In that moment, Julieta came out of her room like a gust of wind. "Talking about favorite girls? Here I am!" She laughed. "You ladies ready to go?"

My sister looked like a teen winter princess out of a

shopping catalog, gift bags dangling from her arms and all. I blew the hair out of my face. Why didn't my hair look like that, vibrant and alive? When I tried to curl it like hers, the edges bunched up in tight curls along my hairline like the crimped edge of an empanada before collapsing like wet paper towels.

Beli and Mami beamed at her. And who could blame them? Juli was the most stylish seventeen-year-old in our whole town of Andromeda. She was popular, relatively nice for being so spoiled, and so smart she was still trying to choose from a handful of colleges that were sure to accept her. I was candlelight, and she was the sun.

"Where are you going?" I asked, and took another sip of hot cocoa. The steam warmed my frozen face, but just barely.

"Mami, Beli, and I are going on a special mission."

"To do what?" I asked, but what I really wanted to know was why they hadn't invited me.

"We're doing random acts of kindness," Julieta said. "Delivering anonymous presents to people who might be feeling lonely during the holidays."

"Anoma-what?" I asked, my eyes going from Mami to Beli. Now I noticed that Mami had changed out of her pajamas while I'd been dealing with the garbage situation. She'd even put on makeup and her dangly earrings. Beli looked ready to go on a polar expedition.

Were they really going to leave me alone?

"A-non-y-mous," Julieta repeated. "It's more fun to do nice things for people when they will never know who the giver was. The act of service is its own reward."

"You have a lonely person right here. I'm sick," I said, pointing at my throat.

"Just because we're thinking of other people doesn't mean we don't love you, Nati. Love isn't a pie that runs out when you divide it. You'll survive for an hour on your own."

I groaned, and Julieta sighed like I was the worst pain in the world. Looking at Mami, she said, "See? I told you she wouldn't get it. She's like a walking dark cloud."

"We were perfectly fine before you barged in," I said, and crossed my arms.

Mami and Beli exchanged one of their wordless looks, which meant they'd talked about this—me and my attitude—already.

Juli continued, "Anyway, I'm ready to go. If you want to come, I'd love to have you along. If not, I'll go be kind on my own."

Mami and Beli jumped into action.

"I'm ready!" Mami said, putting on her boots.

"Wait for me!" said Beli, tying one of Papi's Real Salt Lake blue-and-red soccer scarves around her neck. It clashed with her green jacket, but fashion always took a step behind warmth for her.

The three of them stared at me, three drops of water. They had the same dark curly hair, shiny brown eyes, and rich bronze skin that no self-tanner lotion could replicate, no matter how I tried. I looked like Papi, with boring straight hair and paler skin, which turned greenish in the cold winter for the lack of sunshine.

"Are you coming?" Mami asked, and it sounded like she really meant it.

There was a heartbeat of a pause when my tongue got ready to say yes, but then Julieta rolled her eyes.

"No," I said, "I don't feel like spreading . . . randomness."

"Kindness," Julieta said.

Mami shrugged, but instead of insisting that I come along, she started lacing her boots.

Julieta was already heading out to the carport. "Come with me, Beli," she said, grabbing all her bags with one hand and holding Beli's hand with the other. "I have a blanket waiting for you in the car so you'll be comfy."

"Ay, mi niña, always so thoughtful!" She took Juli's arm and then turned to look at me as the cup of cocoa got cold in my hands. "Put some more Vicks VapoRub on your chest, Nati. I promise, one more dose and the froggy throat will be a thing of the past."

Before I replied that Vicks didn't work against older-sister sassiness, Mami came up to me and kissed me on the cheek. I knew it was a trick to make sure I didn't have a fever.

"Lock up and call me if you need anything," she whispered, as if these were secret rules and not what she repeated every day before going out.

Soon, I heard the rumble of the car going away. I finished drinking the cocoa to wash the bitterness off my tongue, and went back to Reuben's messages on the computer. He was offline. His last message had been one of his silly jokes.

I don't think a cat could eat all those chickens unless it was a meowtain lion in disguise.

I only laughed because he wasn't around to see me.

A few minutes later, when I hadn't replied, he'd said, *Get it?*

I laughed even more and dialed his number on the house phone.

On the third ring, a horrible howling sound made me freeze, as if I were one of the icicles hanging from the gutters. I perked up to listen. It sounded like the crying of a demon baby, and something else, hissing and growling back.

The noise came from the shed. I ran to the window to see what was happening, but it was darker now that the snow had started falling. Under the dim glow of the neighbors' light, I could just make out a raccoon standing in front of the shed door. I had left it open after all! If that raccoon ransacked Mami's things, I'd be grounded until the end of the world. But why wasn't it going in?

Then I saw the small cat blocking the raccoon's path, arching its back as if it were trying to make itself look bigger and more menacing.

"Hello! Hello," Reuben's voice blared from the phone.

It scared me so badly, I shrieked and dropped the phone. It bounced once on the tiled kitchen floor, and then the battery flew out from the back, cutting Reuben's frantic voice off.

The cat howled again, and when I looked up through the window, I saw the raccoon lunge at it. I didn't think. I grabbed the broom from the closet and ran out of the house in my slippers. The snow seeped through the thin fabric and burned my naked skin. I screamed at the top of my lungs, half because of the cold, and half trying to scare off the raccoon.

As soon as it heard me coming, the raccoon ran away from me, across the street, and into the Rogerses' bushes. The cat darted into the darkness of the shed.

I had to shoo the cat away before I locked up. In spite of the cold, sweat prickled under my arms. When I found the hanging electric cord with the light switch in the middle of the room, I was panting. This wasn't the moment for a meltdown. I had to keep my wits, or what was left of them.

I pulled on the cord and the air reverberated with energy. It took a few seconds for my eyes to adjust to the brightness of the light bulb.

"Gato?" I called.

More silence, and then I heard a tiny meow.

I followed the sound all the way to the old armoire, where Mami kept old coats and baby toys. My chest heaved as I stood in front of the semi-closed door.

"Are you there, kitty?" I asked, moving the coats aside.

At the sound of my voice, the cat's tiny face popped out from the coats and jackets, startling me.

"Hey," I said, relieved it didn't look ferocious like when it was fighting the raccoon. But then my attention flickered to the rest of the cat. At its feet were several tiny . . . creatures. My mind struggled to count, but there were a bunch. They were all different colors. Pink, whitish, multi-colored, and striped, but the one thing they had in common was long pink tails.

Mice?!

The cat lay curled in a crescent moon position and, with a swift move of its arm, gathered the creatures close to its tummy.

"What's going on?" I whispered.

The cat blinked its yellow eyes slowly, and then I understood.

Kittens. The cat and the raccoon had been fighting over newborn kittens.

Chapter 2
Meeting the Destruction

The cat had babies in our storage shed. The cat had babies!

I peered at her closely to make sure the mama wasn't hurt after her fight with the raccoon. She was purring loudly as her babies nuzzled against her tummy. The kittens were nursing just like the piglets I'd seen at the state fair last year.

"You're a mama gata," I said in awe, and I don't know why, but my eyes prickled, and my throat throbbed, but I didn't think it was because of the virus.

The cat blinked again, and I imagined it thinking, *Finally. It took you a while, but you understood! Now, help us!*

I wanted to help her, but what did she need?

I stretched out my hand to pet her head. Last time, the cat had run away from me, and now I was afraid that she'd hiss or scratch me. She did none of that. Instead, she closed her eyes and kept purring while my hand caressed her soft fur. The purring was an electric current that went all the way to my heart. There was no explanation for the impossible idea taking ahold of my mind.

I had to bring them inside. I had to protect these kittens, including the mom, until they were old enough to fend for themselves.

My heart started pounding again. I couldn't leave this little family out in the cold. The shed's temperature would only drop in the night, and the kittens and their mom would freeze to death. In the best-case scenario, they'd survive the worst of winter and I'd be able to keep them here in secret. But what about the raccoon?

Even if the mama kept her babies safe from harm, I was sure *my* mom wouldn't be happy when in the next few weeks she started seeing a bunch of wild cats hanging in the shed with her precious craft supplies. I didn't need to be an expert on cats to know that if the kittens grew up away from humans and became wild, they'd never find families who'd adopt them.

My mom would never let me keep the cats in the house, though. Once, Papi had wanted to get one, but she'd complained that a group of cats is called a *destruction* for a reason. I had no idea what she was basing her accusations on because we'd never had a pet before. But what was the right thing to do? I couldn't go back inside and pretend I didn't know about the cat family.

I had to act now.

If only Reuben were here to tell me what to do! If only I hadn't dropped the phone! But I couldn't waste time with what-ifs. The snow was falling fast, and soon the flurries could turn into a blizzard. I didn't have much time.

I had to find something to carry the cat family in, but what? It's not as if the shed was a Room of Requirement like in the Harry Potter books, but among all the junk, there had to be something I could use.

While the cat watched me, I searched around and finally grabbed one of the transparent plastic containers where I kept my favorite samples of slime. I emptied it, pushing the tubs of slime under an old chair with my foot. I'd have to come back later to organize my secret stash, but now I had no time to lose.

Once I had emptied the bin, I lined it with a couple of the old baby blankets no one would ever use again, and said, "Let's go home, mamacat."

The cat didn't understand me the same way I understood her. She just lay there and looked at me. Should I go ahead and grab the kittens? Once, when I was like four, Julieta and I had found baby birds that'd fallen out of the nest. She'd warned me not to touch them because the mom would smell the scent of humans on them and reject them. I'd run to the kitchen to get paper towels to pick them up.

Later on, Papi had said that was a myth, but who'd asked birds for their take on the topic? What if it was true that the animal mom rejects her babies if humans touch them? I couldn't take the risk.

I'd seen a couple mismatched mittens by the coats, so on impulse, I grabbed them, put them on, and picked up one of the sleeping kittens. I carefully placed it in the bin.

The mamacat's hair along her spine bristled, but I stood super still so she'd know I didn't mean her or the babies any harm. Just when I couldn't hold my breath any longer, she grabbed the smallest baby by the scruff of the neck and took it inside the bin to join the kitten already there. She went back for another one, and I gently moved the remaining two. They were five velvety balls of the softest yarn ever, light and fragile. A rapid heartbeat drummed against the palm of my hand. It was strong and steady.

I imagined it sang, *I'm here. I'm here. Help me. Help me.*

Once the kittens were all tucked inside the bin, the mamacat meowed at me as if asking what was next. I picked her up. She was surprisingly light. I could feel her ribs poking out. Carefully, I placed her next to her babies. Their tiny cries sounded like little squeak toys. She licked them vigorously and they calmed down.

"Hold on tight, amigos," I said, my voice shrill with excitement. "We're going home."

The mamacat stared at me like she trusted I wouldn't let her down. That look gave me strength to lift the bin. I gauged its weight. It wasn't that heavy. I could do this.

Then I turned off the light, closed the door so the raccoon wouldn't be able to get inside, and headed back toward my house.

I walked as fast as I could through the snowdrifts toward the bright lights of the kitchen, readjusting the awkward bin every few steps. I didn't want to jostle the babies. They had to be newborns, like, born today, within the last few hours. I'd been in the shed all day yesterday and hadn't seen or heard them, and the tiny meows were impossible to confuse for something else.

My feet were numb with the cold and my ears hurt. I tried to move fast so the little family wouldn't get snowed on.

The kitchen light shone like a bonfire. One more step. Now another.

I hadn't quite latched the door, so I shoved it open, my

arms shaking, and the plastic edge biting through the mittens into the palms of my hands. The mamacat kept her golden eyes on me. The babies meowed fitfully. As carefully as I could, I placed the bin on the floor in the middle of the kitchen. I was shivering just from being outside that long, so the cats must have been cold too.

Without really knowing what was guiding me, I took the mittens off and grabbed another blanket from the chair where Mami had been working. I placed it on top of the bin to keep them warm. Why hadn't I done that before I tried to cross from the shed? The cat was fiercely licking the five babies again. She looked at me as if she wanted to tell me something.

Then it fell on me. She *was* telling me she had to keep them warm! I looked around the kitchen, trying to figure out how I could help her.

For starters, turn on the space heater. I ran to get it from Beli's room. On the bed, she'd left her hot-water bottle, and I grabbed it on the fly. She'd need it to warm her feet tonight, but this was an emergency. I placed the heater next to the bin; I filled the bottle and wrapped it in a kitchen towel, and I placed it in a corner of the bin.

The mamacat huddled around the warmth with her babies. Poor thing, she was frantic. One water bottle wasn't enough! I had to improvise. The memory of a YouTube life hacks video flashed in my mind. I grabbed a couple old socks from the giant lost sock bag in the laundry, filled them with rice, and put them in the microwave for a couple minutes. The mamacat mewed as I tucked in the makeshift heat packs.

"You're welcome," I said, and my voice sounded hoarse.

Soon, I'd have to reheat the warm packs and refill the water bottle, but for now they seemed to work. The adrenaline started leaving my body, and as I got warmer, my hands and feet began throbbing with pain. I was shaking like green Jell-O in the school cafeteria. But I didn't have time to think about myself when the kittens had just escaped death. I wasn't going to lose them now.

Once I stopped breathing fast, I drank a glassful of water. Maybe the cat was thirsty too? I found a shallow dish, filled it with water, and put it next to her inside the bin. All the babies were safe, but before drinking, she checked on them again. She was a good mama! She lapped the water with her dainty pink tongue to the last drop. When she finished, she looked at me, asking for more. Poor mamacat. How long had it been since she'd had a drink? I'd fed her once and she'd been desperate enough to leave her kittens to go rummage in the garbage for more food, but in the cold, she'd probably not been able to find fresh water on her own.

While she drank, I brought her another can of tuna, the kind with the pop-up lid.

The computer dinged with an incoming message. It could only be Reuben.

Ay, pobre! Last he'd heard from me, I'd screamed like a banshee and dropped the phone. Then I'd completely forgotten about him.

Natalia, if you don't answer right this second, I'm calling 9-1-1. What's going on??? Are you alive?

No silly jokes, which told me he was scared. Yikes! This whole thing with the kittens and the raccoon was too fantastic to explain via text. I frantically looked for the phone and found the battery under the couch, and the rest of it hidden under one of Mami's hanging ferns in the kitchen. I put the phone together while another message dinged, and to my relief, when I pressed the call button the signal came right on. I speed-dialed his number, and before it rang once, Reuben picked up.

"What. In. The. World?" he said, sounding like he was speaking through clenched teeth.

I couldn't help it. I laughed, just like I did any time nerves got the best of me, or when a swell of emotion was threatening to take over. But if I cried, Reuben might do something drastic, like come over, or call the authorities.

"Why are you laughing?" Now he sounded like I'd hurt his feelings.

"Reuben, are you sitting down?" I bit my lip to prevent myself from laughing again. "What I'm about to tell you is stranger than fiction."

Without going into a lot of details, I told him what had just happened.

"Wow, I mean, meow," Reuben said.

"What do I do now?" I asked, glancing over my shoulder at the kittens. I wondered where my family was. How long could random, anonymous service take? Were they okay? I'd have to call them and make sure, but that would have to wait until I devised a plan for my cats. "I fed the mamacat and gave her water. She keeps licking the babies . . . but what else am I missing that would mean life or death?"

Reuben sighed, and I could picture his freckle-splattered nose scrunching up as he thought. "Well, I'm not a cat person, so I don't know. But to start, I'm sure the mama will need a litter box. Let me find out what else. I have the knowledge of humankind at the tip of my fingers."

I could hear the click of the keyboard as he typed, and I sighed with relief. If there was any crucial information I needed to know, he'd find it. For now, I needed something that would work as a litter box. My eyes zeroed in on Mami's supplies. I grabbed a shallow box that had contained jars, and a bag of sand that she'd been using for mini succulent terrariums. I wasn't sure this was what cats used for a bathroom, but I hoped it worked for now.

Reuben kept muttering to himself, and in the meantime, I walked over to the bin. All the babies were so cute, my hands itched with wanting to pick them up and cuddle them. Under the bright kitchen light, I could see their proper colors. Two were a grayish-white, one was orange, one was black-and-white, and one, the tiniest one of all, was all colors splashed together, like a rainbow kitten, with a black-and-white body and orange-and-white-striped legs.

"How old are these babies?" he asked with more clicking in the background.

"I haven't asked them, but I'm guessing they're hours old," I said. "They weren't in the shed yesterday."

Reuben laughed, and then said, "The most important thing is to keep them warm, then, and make sure the mama is comfortable. Don't really touch them until they're two days old. At least. I'm not kitting."

I snatched my hand away. I had just been about to pick

up the rainbow one. Outside, a car rumbled past, and I held my breath to hear if it was Julieta's car, but then the sound faded. I needed time to prepare for when they came home.

"But really, the most important thing is to take them to the vet," Reuben said.

There was a silence as I tried to figure out how to get them there, and then he gasped.

"What?" I asked, my heart jumping.

"Call the shelter! They'll know what to do. They have vets and volunteers and stuff."

"The shelter? In every movie and show, the shelter is literally the worst place to send an animal. They kill them there."

Reuben clicked his tongue. "You watch too many old movies," he said. "They love animals there, and they'll do anything to save the kittens. Really, I wish shows would stop making them the bad guys when all they do is try to help."

"Reuben! Get off the phone and the computadora! Too

much time with electrónicos, chamo!" It was his mom's voice blaring all the way to my side of the line. Like ours, his family was fluent in Spanglish.

Reuben groaned on the phone, but when he replied, his voice was chill. "Coming, Mom!"

I covered the phone so he wouldn't hear me laughing. And really, why was I laughing? When my mom came back, I'd get an earful.

"Listen," Reuben said, "call the shelter and ask them what to do. Trust me. They close at eight. Here's the number."

I wasn't a hundred percent sure that calling the shelter was a good idea, but Reuben had never led me in the wrong direction. In fact, if I'd paid attention to his warnings about the exclusive customer lottery, Slime Supreme would still be thriving and Meera wouldn't have betrayed me. Most importantly, I wouldn't have the reputation of being *the* mean girl of Andromeda Elementary. I wrote the number down.

"Got it?" Reuben asked.

"Yeah. I'll call them."

"Good. Keep me in the loop. I'll come over tomorrow morning to help you."

"Come over early," I whined. "No sleeping till noon. I'll need you!"

"Yes, ma'am!" he said, and when I was about to hang up, he added, "Ah! Take pictures. You must document everything. Remember what Meera always used to say."

He was gone before I could tell him off for bringing Meera up.

Reuben was right, though. Meera was the queen of social media, and the slime business had exploded once she'd helped me with pictures, videos, and graphics. When I watched the hypnotizing five-second videos of slime being swirled into a container, I had wanted to buy my own confections. Then she'd ruined everything . . . but the videos were still cool.

Now, for documenting. I needed a phone to get video and pictures! But I didn't have a phone or even a tablet. My mind went into overdrive. I could wait until my family was back and ask one of them to lend me a device, but never again would I have this moment of peace and quiet with the mamacat and her babies. Who knew what Mami would decide once she arrived home?

If only there was a way to take pictures that didn't require a phone . . . And then I realized I didn't need a phone. I needed a camera.

Julieta had an old-fashioned one in her closet that her dad had given her. Her room was out of bounds, but when had she used her camera last? Why would she care if I used it? This was a true emergency, and besides, in all my years of getting in trouble, I'd learned that it was easier to ask for forgiveness than for permission.

Her door was locked, but hers was a simple cylinder lock I could open with a flat knife. In less than a minute, I was in. I grabbed the camera from her closet, and once I figured out how it worked, I started snapping pictures of the cats. Their adorable noses and feet were unreal. I tried to touch them as little as possible, but I noticed the tiniest one was the only one not nursing. It was off to a side, sleeping.

A horrible fear came over me. What if . . . ? Gently, I placed my index finger on the baby's back. It was hardly breathing. It needed help! I picked it up and placed it close to the mom's tummy. It started nursing, but it stopped too soon, as if it were too tired to eat.

This kitten didn't look too good. My heart started pounding like when I'd been lugging the bin.

Could the kittens have been born too early? I'd been pre-mature, and spent weeks in the newborn intensive care unit, the NICU. Every November on my birthday, Mami took out my baby photo album and told me stories of how if it hadn't been for the extra help, I wouldn't have made it.

Frantically, I looked around as if a fairy cat-mother would pop out of thin air to tell me what to do. I didn't see one, of course. Instead, I saw the kitchen clock marking seven forty-five.

The shelter closed at eight!

I put the camera away in my room to use it later and called the shelter.

Chapter 3
Cat Saviors

"Andromeda Cat Rescue, how may I help you?"

I cleared my throat before I answered. "Oh, hi. I'm calling because I found a cat that had babies, and I was wondering what I should do. There's six counting the mom."

The woman groaned. "Really? I had a call about a litter of babies this morning, and another yesterday. Kitten season isn't even supposed to be until March, but I guess when it rains it pours, right?"

My face felt like it was on fire even though I hadn't done anything wrong. Calling had been a total mistake. I sat on the floor next to the plastic bin. I'd have to find a better place to put the cats. The walls were too high for the mom to leave easily to go to the bathroom and eat.

The woman must have regretted her tone of voice because she added, "I'm sorry, sweetheart, you did the right thing. All we do at our shelter is rescue little ones. Thanks for calling, really, but we're far over capacity. Most of my volunteers are out of town for the holidays. If the kittens were older, I'd be able to take them, but when they're that small, they're a lot of work. I just don't have the resources or the necessary cat rescuers."

My heart grew heavy. "So you just let them die?" I asked, my voice louder than was polite.

After a few seconds of awkward silence, the woman asked, "You said they're with the mom, right?"

"Yes, and she's a good mama," I said, petting the mama-cat's head. "There's a small one that's struggling to eat. What should I do?"

The woman sighed in the way that's never followed by good news. "She might be okay, but it'd be ideal if you took them to a vet," she said, and I could tell she was trying to sound nice. "The vet can give you kitten replacement milk to supplement. She'll also be able to check that the kittens don't have fleas and ear mites."

"Ear mites?" I said, putting a hand over my free ear.

"Just to make sure. If you have internet access, check for kitten care videos. There are a lot of resources online. Other than that, I'm afraid we can't really help you at the moment." Her voice sounded honestly pained.

My mind was whirling. My mom had a soft heart; maybe she would let them stay. But if Mami even suspected the cats might have creepy-crawlies, she wouldn't be happy.

"In a couple weeks, we could take them, but for now, you'd have to foster them like our volunteers would," the woman said. "Do you think you could do that?"

I hesitated for a few seconds. I had never taken care of any newborn being ever, but the mamacat seemed to know what to do. I had no other option. "Yes, I do," I finally said. "And I'll check with the vet. Thank you."

She sighed, sounding relieved. "Fostering can be a lot of

work. So make sure you include the whole family. Good luck," she added, before she softly hung up.

I thought of the work ahead of me. Taking care of kittens wasn't something I'd imagined in a million years, especially not during winter break. But honestly, if it was going to happen, this was the best timing ever. I'd be home all day for the next ten days. When school started, and especially after Beli left in a couple weeks, then that would be another story. I'd have to think about it later. Like the lady had suggested, I could include my whole family in this project.

I looked inside the bin at the small one and said, "You hang in there, chiquitito."

The mama was licking it vigorously, like giving it a rub-down. Again. She was spending so much time on this one. At least she seemed to know what to do. I hoped it would be enough until the vet could check them.

I looked online for the closest animal hospital and wrote down the address on a Post-it. The place was just on Main Street, and it would be open until midnight. I wondered how expensive the vet would be, and if I had enough money to pay. Good thing I had some savings from Slime Supreme. Usually there had been nothing left over after I bought supplies, but after my last batch was sold, Mami hadn't let me buy any more slime ingredients. So I'd kept the money safe in my underwear drawer, where I went to dig it out. Just as I pulled the bag from the back of the drawer, I heard the sound of someone opening the side door.

"Ay caramba!" I exclaimed as I rushed back out to the bin in the kitchen. The cats were all huddled together, even the tiny one.

Maybe I should've planned better, hiding them in the bathroom or something until I could prepare my mom, but now it was too late. Mami, Beli, and Julieta were walking in, and by the sound of it, Mami wouldn't be too eager to head back out in the cold night to drive the cats to the vet.

"I just want to sit in front of the TV and do nothing for the rest of the night," she said. "Ah! Warmth at last!"

The three of them saw me at the same time. Julieta's nose shone bright pink, and under other circumstances I would've mentioned how on point she was with the season, looking like the famous reindeer and all. But for once, I held my tongue. Six feline lives depended on the crucial following seconds.

Mami looked at me, then at the bin at my feet. "What's going on?" Her urgent tone frightened me. "What happened?"

"Mami," I started saying, but then the mamacat peeked out of the bin as if she wanted to see who was talking. Beli and Juli saw the cat at the same time. Their reactions couldn't have been more different. Julieta screamed like la Llorona, and Beli exclaimed, "Un gatito? Ay, qué cute!" and walked briskly to me, her scarf trailing behind her. When she saw what was in the tub, she gasped and covered her mouth with her hands.

"Six gatitos!" she mumbled.

"Gatitos?" my mom shrieked. "Mami, for the love of summer, what do you mean?"

"Shhh," I said, not necessarily shushing my mom and my sister, but calming the mamacat, whose back was bristled up, prepared to attack these loud, menacing humans.

When I didn't reply, Mami came over and looked down at the bin. Melting snow was already pooling at her feet. It was proof of how unexpected this was for her that she hadn't even taken her boots off or demanded that Beli and Julieta do the same.

Mami was speechless. She just looked at me.

"I found them in the shed," I said, standing between the cats and my mom. "There *was* a raccoon, and it was after them, Mami. What was I supposed to do? I couldn't let it eat the poor creatures."

My heart pounded in my ears, and my throat felt so tight I couldn't breathe right.

"Ay, mi amor," Mami sighed, plopping on the sofa in the living room. She put her hands through her long hair, which was wet and plastered on her head. "Cats? Six of them!"

"I hate cats!" said Julieta. "They're like vampires with their claws and fangs. And all the hair!"

"They're tiny," I said in an even tinier voice.

Beli was kneeling next to the tub, petting the mamacat's

head. This was progress. My mom hardly ever said no to my sister, but to Beli? Anything my grandma said was the law.

"Let me explain," I said in the calmest voice I could manage.

To her credit, Julieta didn't interrupt me. Instead, after a cautious look at the kittens, she put the kettle on, and while I told the story of how I'd found the cats, she made hot chocolate for all, even for me.

Not wanting to ruin the moment, I left out crucial details, like how I had fed the mamacat the day before, and how I'd left the shed door open because I'd been in there playing with the slime. Mami was smart, and eventually she'd put two and two together. For now, I needed time and the chance to prove I could help these poor gatos.

"Did the raccoon bite the cat?" Beli asked when I told them about the fight.

"I . . . I don't think so," I said, worried about the tone of her voice. "I checked all of them, and they don't have a single scratch."

Beli looked at Mami and said, "Still, it wouldn't be a bad idea to have the poor innocent animals checked by a vet, Gina. Just in case. Besides, look at this little one. It's too small."

Even without looking, I knew which kitten Beli was talking about.

Mami and Beli shared one of those wordless looks.

"It needs help just like I needed help when I was born, Mami," I said, and even Julieta looked mortified. I might have been the one who spent weeks in the NICU, but it was my family, including my sister, who ended up with the painful memories.

Again, Mami put her hands on her head. "I wasn't planning on going out again tonight," she said in a tired voice. "I have to work early tomorrow!"

I looked down at my hands. This was the worst part of being a kid. I couldn't expect Mami to go to work with no sleep. Beli didn't drive, especially not in the snow. I was at the mercy of my sister.

"I see you used the baby blankets I'd been saving,

Natalia," Mami said, and she totally sounded like she was whining. "And Beli's hot-water bottle!"

"Sorry, Mami," I said. "I grabbed the first things I found. They would've died. They still could die. I called the shelter, and the woman there said they're full, but that the vet could help, and—"

"You called the shelter?" Mami asked. "What did they say?"

"They're swamped. They don't have enough volunteers."

Mami's shoulders slumped. "Why does trouble always find you, Natalia?"

I didn't know what to say.

Julieta and Beli sat next to Mami, in front of me. The silence was unbearable, until Mami took another deep breath.

"Mira, Natalia," she finally said, and I braced myself. This was it. Her final decision. "It's late. I had one of the longest days of my life, and I'm grateful to be back in my warm home. I'm not a monster, so I won't kick out these poor animals—" I gasped, excited, and she added, "Let me finish! Yet. I won't kick them out yet. But why don't you wait until tomorrow to take them to the vet?"

The excitement died as soon as it had been born. Maybe most of the kittens could wait until tomorrow, but the tiny one couldn't. I bit my lip to stop myself from arguing, and when I looked up, I saw Julieta looking at me in a way that made my eyes fill with tears for some reason. It wasn't a mean look; it was actually as if she were seeing the real me for the first time in a long time, since before we started fighting over Mami's attention, when I was my sister's treasure and she was my everything.

"I'll drive her," Julieta said, and it took me a second to understand her words. "What if they have fleas or something? I won't be able to sleep until we know they're not carrying a disease anyway."

Mami and Beli sent Julieta one of those adoring looks, and she shrugged like it wasn't a big deal being this perfect.

"Thank you," I said, and to my surprise, it came out without any snark. Too much hung in the balance.

Beli stood up slowly, as if every joint in her body hurt.

She kissed my forehead and ruffled my hair. "You're a cat hero tonight," she whispered.

"Drive safely, Julieta," Mami said, and then she looked at me. "Do you know where to go?"

I showed her the Post-it with the address, and my ziplock bag with my money. Surprise flashed across Mami's face. She looked at Julieta and said, "Gracias for doing this, mi amor. Drive slowly. You don't need another flat tire."

"Flat tire?" I asked.

Julieta huffed and said, "It's a long story. Ready to go?"

Without wasting time, I picked up the bin and headed out, my sister following me. I stood next to the door, and Julieta got the hint and opened the side door and then the car door for me. The car was still warm, and we drove the few blocks to the vet while Julieta told me about their flat tire and the strangers who'd helped them get home.

"Anonymous strangers?" I asked.

"You know Beli. After five minutes, she knew their whole life story. She got their address so we can bring them quesitos, or chocolate chip cookies maybe."

Nothing she said surprised me.

Maybe the cat angels were looking out for us, because the whole way to Main Street, we drove behind a snowplow, which turned in time for Julieta to pull into the Andromeda Animal Hospital. Once upon a time, the hospital had been a cottage, and now it looked all cozy blanketed in snow, a little light in each window.

Before I unbuckled my seat belt, Julieta said, "I'll go in and let them know you have young kittens. In case there's a dog in the front office."

How did she always know the perfect thing to do? Was she born like this, or had she learned? If she'd learned, when would all the knowledge drop on me?

She dashed in, and good thing, because through the cracked door, I could see there was a large dog in the front office. It barked as soon as Julieta went in.

At first, I was startled by the sound that reverberated in my ears even though I was in the car. But then I recognized the dog. My sister knelt down to pet him, none other than Captain America.

Chapter 4
The Circle of Life

Waiting in the car was agony, but soon a woman in scrubs came out and helped me carry the bin inside. At that moment, another nurse was leading Cap to a small room off the reception area.

"Your family's waiting for you, friend," she said in a cheerful voice that clashed with the mood in the room.

The old dog could hardly walk, and his superhero cape hung to one side, all crooked. But he still wagged his tail when he entered the room and several people whispered his name with affection. It sounded like all of Meera's family was gathered: Meera, her parents and grandparents, and her little brother, Bodhi, who cried loudly.

What were they all doing here? Was Cap sick? He'd seemed like his normal self earlier today.

"Old Cap is saying goodbye to the world tonight," the nurse at the reception desk whispered, guessing my questions. "He's had a good life."

I gasped and had to set the bin on the ground before I dropped it. Julieta's eyes were shiny with tears, and she sniffed on her pink sweater sleeve. The Rogerses had always joked that Cap was immortal; he'd already been very old when Meera's dad got him from a rescue when we were in kindergarten. The whole neighborhood knew him and loved him. Now his time had really come. Meera and her brother would be devastated.

"Let me take the bin from you," the lady said, interrupting my thoughts. "Come with me."

We followed her to a small observation room.

When the nurse, whose scrubs had a print of kittens posing as the letters of the alphabet, uncovered the bin and saw the mamacat and her babies, her face broke up in the sweetest smile. "Look at you!" And then she turned to me and said, "The circle of life, huh? Old Cap is reaching the end, and these little guys are just starting out."

Julieta kept sniffling in a corner, and I walked up to the observation table to reassure the mamacat that everything would be all right.

"This one's very small," the nurse whispered, massaging the tiny kitten's back. "Much smaller than the rest. Let me call Dr. Michael."

She left the room right away. I looked into the bin, and to my horror saw the tiny one was very still.

"No!" I said. My first impulse was to pick it up, but I remembered Reuben's words. "Hold on, chiquitito. Hold on," I whispered.

Julieta patted my shoulder without saying a word. Her speechlessness was what worried me the most. Usually she came up with something positive to say about every situation. Now she had nothing.

Luckily the vet came into the room when the knot in my throat threatened to turn into tears. He smiled, but I could tell he was sad, maybe because Cap was crossing the bridge to dog heaven. Because if there really was a heaven for pets, then he'd earned his wings and more. My eyes prickled thinking of him and, honestly, of Meera losing her friend.

The vet's shirt looked a little rumpled, as if he'd been at work all day. Mami complained that us girls always got sick during the holidays; maybe it was the same with animals.

"What do we have here?" he asked.

I pointed at the tiny baby curled in a corner of the bin like the tiniest yarn ball.

His face softened when he picked it up. His gloves were light purple. "So small!" he said, and it sounded like he was trying not to squeal like everyone else when they saw the babies.

In the meantime, the nurse had prepared the scale, and carefully, the doctor deposited the kitten on it. The numbers flashed and finally settled on 60.

The lady shook her head and made a note on her clipboard.

One by one, the doctor weighed each of the babies. They were all much heavier than the first one, their weights ranging from 90 to 110.

"Are those ounces?" I asked. Math was my kryptonite, but even I knew those weren't pounds.

The vet's mustache twitched. "Those are grams; each kitten is about three ounces. Grams are more accurate in small creatures like these fluffballs."

"Oh my gosh! I never knew kittens were so tiny when they were born!" Julieta said.

The vet smiled more widely. "Actually, these kittens are way smaller than average. Even the biggest one, this gray one, is on the smallish range of birth weight. Newborn kittens should weigh anywhere from eighty to a hundred and seventy grams at birth, and I'd say these babies were born within the day, right?" He'd put all the babies back with their mama but kept the tiny one in his hands.

"I found them a few hours ago," I said, not taking my eye from the small one, now wrapped in a towel like a burrito and mewing weakly. The sound was so small and fragile, but at least it was something.

The vet rubbed the baby vigorously with the towel, and another vet tech came in and handed him the smallest baby bottle I'd seen in my life. It was a mixture of bottle and syringe actually.

"Tell me how you found them," he said, putting the nipple to the baby's mouth. The kitten nuzzled but didn't seem to know what to do. The vet trickled some milk into its mouth, and when it realized what the mystery liquid was, the kitten started suckling hungrily. The vet smiled, satisfied.

A little more relieved, I told the story again, but this time, I got carried away and accidentally let slip the fact that I had fed the mother yesterday.

At this, Julieta sent me an accusing look, and with cheeks on fire, I tried to ignore her and continue my tale.

When I reached the end, Dr. Michael said, "You did an excellent job." I lit up like fireworks were exploding inside me. "You saved their lives."

I glanced at Julieta, who finally smiled. For once, I'd known what to do and I'd done it right.

"This tiny girl here," the vet continued, "needs all the help she can get."

"The mama?" I asked.

"Yes, the mama is a very young cat herself to be a queen."

"Queen?"

The vet smiled, and I didn't know if it was because I kept repeating what he said. "Female cats are called queens when they have kittens," he said. "When they give birth, it's called queening. And she's the smallest and youngest queen I've met in a long time. She only weighs six pounds, which is too little for a mother cat. She can't be older than seven or eight months. Poor girl."

I didn't know how cat years compared to human years, but she did look way small and young to me.

"What does she need?" Julieta asked.

"If you're planning on keeping them at least until the babies can be placed with families, she should be on a weight-gaining nutritional plan. This little kitten needs to be supplemented until she catches up to her siblings, or at least until she's within the normal weight range."

The vet flipped through the clipboard and the notes the nurse had taken.

"Have you called the local shelter? The babies should remain with their mom until they're at least eight weeks. Sometimes the shelter can take the whole family in, but sadly, they have more animals to take care of than people who volunteer. Their resources are so few, and they can't take every animal that needs help."

I nodded. "They *are* full. They can't take the kittens now because they don't have enough volunteers to foster."

"Shelters do all they can do," the nurse said. I glanced at her name tag, which said her name was Susan. "Shelter workers and volunteers are heroes. And now you're one too. Kittens are cute, but of course, they grow up. There are too many homeless animals." She waved a flat device over the mamacat.

"What's that for?" I asked to change the subject. I'd liked how she called me a hero, but anyone would have done the same in my situation, I thought.

"To see if she's microchipped. Maybe when the owners realized she was pregnant, they abandoned her. People dump their unwanted animals in the mountains all the time, thinking they'll fend for themselves," the vet said.

"That's so mean," said Julieta.

The vet laughed, but he didn't sound amused. "Yes, mean and irresponsible, because in most cases, the animals just die. They can't fend for themselves. Or maybe this mama cat slipped out of the house and didn't know how to go back. Maybe there's a family looking for her. Who knows? A lot of people are gone for the holidays, and sometimes pet sitters lose track of their charges."

I hadn't considered that the cat had a family. What if she did? What if right now, a girl just like me was crying because she couldn't find her pet? My mind sped wildly through possible scenarios, but I shooed them away.

That girl should've done a better job at taking care of her cat, especially one about to become a queen, a mother of kittens.

The vet interrupted my thoughts. "Nothing came up on the scan, so she's not microchipped, or if she is, it's malfunctioning. If you want, we can put up a sign here at the office and on our social media pages. Maybe someone will reply with more information."

My heart pounded in my throat. I didn't want to lose her. I didn't want anyone to take her away from me.

"When they call, how can we know they're really telling the truth? What if they're horrible pet owners, and she ran away?" Suddenly, all the grown-ups and Julieta were looking at me, and I fidgeted in place.

"I promise that before I make any decision, I'll be one hundred percent sure it's the best course of action for the mama and the babies," the vet said. "But it won't hurt to ask around. What do you think?"

The vet's was a sensible idea, so without a way out, I nodded.

"We'll call you if anyone answers our ad," the nurse, Susan, said. Then she looked at me and asked, "By the way, what are you calling her so we can put it in our records?"

Her question was the most important one of the night. I loved naming things. For example, my slime had been good, but part of what got people addicted to it was the names. I tried to look all calm, but on the inside, I was doing cartwheels. I hadn't thought of a name for the cats before, but still, the thought process took less than a second. In my mom's family, everyone had a name related to royalty. Mami was Regina, Beli's name was really Isabel. My middle name was Victoria, and Julieta's was Sofia. Since mother cats are queens, it was only natural that she also got a royal name.

"Queen Georgiana," I said. "Gigi for short."

The mamacat looked at me and blinked once in that way that I had started to understand meant yes. Julieta nodded approvingly, and I couldn't stop a smile from creeping onto my face when Susan wrote it down on the form.

In the meantime, the vet was looking at the kittens' ears and tummies. He had a sweet smile on his face, so I assumed he wasn't finding anything to worry about.

"No fleas or ear mites?" I asked.

"Cats have ear mites?" Julieta said, covering her ears.

The vet smiled again and said, "They can, but these kittens look totally clean."

Susan squirted some medicine into every feline mouth, including Gigi's. "Dewormer," she explained.

My sister and I shared a look of horror and disgust.

"I took a blood sample from them to make sure they're healthy, and especially because I'm curious about this one," the vet said, showing me the tiny rainbow kitten, which was now asleep and breathing deep with its full tummy.

"Why are you curious?" asked Juli.

The vet smiled widely and said, "I have a suspicion that she's a chimera. See?" He showed us her legs, striped orange-and-white. "She looks like two kittens mashed up."

"I think she looks like a rainbow," I said.

"But what does it mean?" Juli asked.

The vet shrugged. "Not much, other than her gene sequence is cool. Ah! And do you want to know what sex the rest of them are?"

"Yes!" I said, thrilled.

He pointed at the bigger ashy gray. "This is a boy. The other gray is a girl. The orange one is a girl, which is kind of rare. Eighty percent of orange cats are male. The black-and-white is a boy, and this possible chimera is a girl. In any case, like her mama, she's a calico. Although, the mom looks like a tortoiseshell when you see her from behind; then in front she has all that white."

Gigi's eyes were trained on the vet, as if she knew he was talking about her. When she noticed we'd noticed her noticing, she turned her face and gave him a side-eye.

We all laughed, and the vet said, "She certainly has the tortitude, you know, the attitude of a tortoiseshell, or torti's attitude."

"She'll fit right in with our family, then," Julieta said, and the vet and Susan laughed. My heart swelled with love for my sister. Did she mean she could see Gigi becoming a permanent member of our family?

The visit felt like it had reached the end, but I hadn't asked something that was worrying me. "So, about the raccoon, it didn't scratch Gigi or the babies. But are they safe? I mean, rabid? She looks calm right now, but I tell you, when she was fighting the raccoon, she was a fury."

The vet chuckled. "She's very docile, which makes me almost sure she had a human family or grew up around people. She will be protective of her babies, so maybe if she gets nervous or scared, she'll overreact, like with the raccoon, which is understandable.

"Respect her wishes if she doesn't want you to touch the babies, but at the same time, they need to be handled starting next week so they'll be ready for their new homes when they're at least eight weeks. Especially the little one. She will cry when she doesn't feel her mom's warmth, so maybe it's safer to give her a bottle away from the mom. Other than that, be careful and gentle."

"Careful and gentle is my expertise," I said, and Julieta pressed her lips like she was trying not to laugh. "Also, is it okay to touch them, or will I need gloves?"

"Only handle the little one for feedings for the next couple days, and then it will be okay to snuggle her and the rest as long as you want."

"Yes!" I exclaimed.

"Okay," the vet said, clapping loudly. Gigi sent him a look and Susan laughed. "I'll give you a discount for today's test since you rescued the babies and the shelter is full. Here's a container of KMR, kitten milk replacer, for the chimera girl and the mama. She needs to put on weight too, and the KMR will help with that. You're good to go now, but I advise that the mama come back to see me in eight weeks for her vaccines and to be fixed so there are no more surprise kittens. They're lovely and adorable, but preventing unwanted births is the responsible way to be a pet owner."

Julieta was about to take her wallet out of her purse, but I said, "I got it," and paid with the remaining money from my business. I'd have to find a way to earn more to support my kittens.

When we left the office, there was no sign of Meera or her family. I wondered how she was feeling now that Cap was gone.

If we'd still been friends, she could have come over to help me with the next stage in my kitten adventure. The kittens would make her happy, or at least make Cap's passing a little easier to shoulder. But there was no way I'd let Meera anywhere near any of my kittens.

Chapter 5
Adorable
Rumpelstiltskin

On the way back home, Julieta drove in silence and I watched the Christmas lights reflected on the new snow. The storm had turned our town into a postcard. The bin with the cats was in the back seat, but I held the tiny kitten next to my heart. She was still wrapped like a kitty burrito, asleep with a full tummy. Now that she was safe, I'd be able to sleep too. That is, for a couple hours, I hoped, until it was time to feed her.

"Are you sure you're up to taking care of the kittens? It will be a lot of work," Julieta said, finally breaking the silence.

"I can do it," I said. "*If* Mami lets me keep them for eight weeks."

Julieta didn't reply. Her silence made my mind go into overdrive. Maybe she didn't want to bash my hopes with a dose of reality.

Eight weeks! That was two months. Sixty days. Now the babies were literally contained, content to only nurse and sleep. I'd seen funny kitten videos, though, and babies grew up to be mischievous kittens, a *destruction*, like Mami had said.

"Thanks for driving me," I said, partly to break the silence and shush the worries in my mind, and more because I really was grateful. "This little one wouldn't have made it. You're really kind, Juli."

"You're welcome," she said, keeping her eyes on the road ahead, but she was smiling.

She was the most responsible seventeen-year-old ever. That's why Mami trusted her with everything and always said yes to her.

My mom always said yes to my sister. I turned to look at her. My mom might not agree to letting me keep the cats. If *I* asked. But if Juli asked? Then I had a good chance.

I didn't know how to bring up the question, but we'd be home soon. I needed her as an ally.

"What?" she asked, a smile still on her face as she eyed me. "You have that look you get when you're plotting something." She put a hand up. "I won't be sacrificing my beauty sleep to feed the babies, so don't even think about it."

"I wasn't going to ask that, though it'd be nice if you helped."

"I already helped you by driving tonight."

It was true, and I couldn't argue with her, so instead I said, "You're right," which took her off guard.

"Now say whatever is on the tip of your tongue or be silent forever."

And they said *I* was dramatic.

Which maybe I was. A little. I took a deep breath to calm my pounding heart. "Will you ask Mami to consider? Please, Juli? To let me keep the cats until they're old enough?"

"Is that all?" She laughed, sarcastically, my least favorite of Julieta's reactions. "That's a lot to ask. Besides, I don't even like cats, remember?"

Julieta might not like cats, but how could she not like the kittens?

"You know how hard it would be for Mami to say yes, Nati Natasha."

Encouraged that she was using my childhood nickname, I hugged the kitten tightly and kissed her tiny folded ears. "Not if you ask."

Silence fell in the car again. I could already see our house and how sad it looked without decorations.

Then, as Julieta was pulling in the driveway, she said, "I'll only agree if you promise something."

"Anything," I said quickly, my hands tingling with anticipation.

"In that case, I want one of the kittens." The reply was too ready on her lips. She'd been thinking about it!

"One of the kittens?" I looked at her through narrowed eyes. "What kind of Rumpelstiltskin request is that?"

To my surprise, Julieta burst into laughter, and not the sarcastic kind. This funny, hiccupping laugh, which was infectious and got everyone around her laughing, was my favorite.

I laughed too. We only recovered when Gigi meowed from the back seat, totally sounding like a mom, and a queen at that.

"Why do you want a kitten?" I asked. "You're going to college in September!"

Beli was waiting by the kitchen window, and she turned around to say something over her shoulder.

Julieta put the car in park and said, "The kitten won't be for me. It'll be for Hayden."

Hayden was Julieta's longtime friend turned boyfriend. Horrible at timing, the both of them, to get together in their senior year. He'd be attending the local college and staying with his parents to save money, and who knew where Julieta would end up? I hoped it wasn't with her dad in California.

The kitchen side door opened, and Beli poked her head and a hand out to signal for us to hurry.

"Promise and I'll convince Mami," Julieta insisted.

Immediately, the connection I'd felt with my sister dissolved. She'd only helped me because she wanted something in return, not out of the kindness of her heart, no matter how much she pretended to be all generous and thoughtful. But beggars can't be choosers, so I gave in.

"Okay," I said, and then added, "But I'll pick which one he can have." I extended my hand for her to shake and seal the deal. She looked at it, and finally shook.

With my sister's help, Mami would agree to let me keep the babies until they were old enough. Then why did I feel like I'd sold my soul?

That night, I was up twice to check on the kittens. The first shift was at two a.m. When I peered into the nest Beli helped me make in a big box with short sides, all the kittens were nursing hungrily, even the tiny rainbow one. On the second turn, at five, the little kitten wanted to sleep as her siblings were eating. But she couldn't miss even one feeding.

Mami got ready to leave for work and watched me in silence as I prepared the syringe bottle. While I sat on the ground and fed the kitten, Mami smiled mysteriously and said, "I sure don't miss the days of getting up at all times of the night for a baby."

I didn't know what I was supposed to say to that, so I didn't say anything.

"The kittens are for sure cute," she said. "Too bad they grow so fast."

It didn't sound like she was talking only about cats now.

"Mami," I said, turning my burning eyes in her direction. I'd stayed up reading cat facts way too late. "At least you only changed diapers. Gigi, the mamacat, actually has to make her babies go potty. It's called stimulation, and she has to . . . you know? Lick their bums so they'll go pee-pee and poo-poo. You know how cats clean up. They don't exactly use a wipe."

Mami didn't laugh like I'd expected. Instead, she shuddered. "Gross!" she said. "And you already named the bigger cat? That's not a good sign, Nati. Don't get attached."

It was too early for a fight. When I was tired and grumpy, the only words that bloomed from the tip of my tongue were sharp ones.

Besides, Mami was leaving soon. Arguing wouldn't help my case. Julieta would have to get going with her part of the deal.

After a few minutes, Mami kissed the top of my head and took a long look at the little kitten. "What are you going to name *her*?"

"I'm not sure yet," I said, a little encouraged by her question. "I wanted a royalty theme. Maybe . . . Victoria? Vicky for short."

Mami shook her head. "That's your middle name! What about Maxima, like the queen of the Netherlands? Max for short. Think about it." She left for work, but by the smile on her face, I got the impression she knew I'd go along with her suggestion.

Later, from the warmth of my bed, enticed by the smell of hot cocoa and sweet bread, I thought the conversation with Mami sounded positive. The more she saw the babies, the more she'd get attached to them. She was strict, but she had a heart.

The sound of laughter made me curious. Who was over

so early? I turned to check the clock. It was eight a.m. I untangled myself from the bedcovers and headed to the kitchen, in a decent mood even with the lack of sleep. My heart fluttered anticipating seeing the kittens.

But the nest wasn't by the couch where I'd left it last. My heart went into drumming mode.

"Where are they?" I asked, looking around and then zooming in on my sister with what I hoped was a smoldering look. Next to her at the kitchen table was Hayden. He was pressing his lips as if trying not to laugh.

Julieta grinned. "You haven't said the magic words, Nati."

I glared at her. "Where are they?"

Finally, Beli came over to me, draped her arm over my shoulder, and said, "Hayden helped me move them to the laundry room, mi amor."

"Why?" I asked, following Beli to the small room off the kitchen, where the nest was on the floor.

"The mom kept moving the babies around," Hayden hollered from the kitchen.

"She did?" I asked Beli, horrified at what could happen if she hid the kittens and I couldn't find them.

"She did! They like quiet and warm places. And look, it's much warmer in here, and if the kittens get used to the room, it'll be easier to keep them contained and safe. They only eat and sleep now, but in a few weeks . . . Your mami agreed that it was best in the long term."

The kittens were nursing, and after one of her hello blinks, Gigi closed her eyes again. Poor mama! If I was sleep deprived, I couldn't imagine how tired she was.

"Breakfast's coming soon," I promised her as I crouched to check on the tiny one, Max, as Mami had named her.

Like her still-nameless siblings, Max was kneading her mama's tummy as she nursed. It reminded me of how Bodhi, Meera's little brother, squeezed his applesauce pouch to extract all the goodness out of it. That had to be a lot of work for such tiny babies.

"They're the cutest things I've seen in my life," Beli said, smiling brightly.

"But what if my mom won't let me keep them, Beli? Can you convince her?"

Beli shook her head, and my heart sank. Then she added, "I believe your sister already put in a good word for you, and you must be asleep still because you didn't realize what I said before."

I leapt to my feet. "Really? When? I saw Mami when she left for work, and she was acting hard to get. You know how she is."

Beli laughed. "You remind me so much of Gina when she was your age; it's like going back in time."

Just when I was going to say I didn't see how the two of us could be even remotely similar, Julieta came to look at the kittens, closely followed by Hayden. Suddenly, I realized he was probably smiling because of my hair, which had a life of its own in the nighttime. I usually woke up with a bird's nest on my head. He didn't seem to notice when I redid my ponytail. Instead, he was looking at the kittens adoringly. It was magical how people's expressions changed when they saw the newborn cats.

"I helped Juli place that makeshift litter box," he said. Although he'd known my sister for years, he still struggled to say her name correctly, the *J* like an *H*. When he said *Juli*, it sounded like *Wooly*. I disguised my laughter into a cough, even though I felt better this morning.

"I had a couple of boxes of litter and a scratching post at home. When Juli told me about the kittens, I thought you might need them more."

"Thanks," I said. "How do you know so much about what cats need?"

Hayden raked his fingers through his shaggy brown hair and said, "Remember Catsby and Bagheera?"

"Who?"

Julieta clicked her tongue. "Remember his cats? Bagheera did this to me in fifth grade." She rolled up her sleeve and showed me three silvery lines along her arm. "It was the first day I went over to your house. Remember, Hay?"

Hayden got a melancholy look in his murky blue eyes. "How could I forget?"

"Best day of my life." If I had to sit and look at Julieta's gooey expression for one more second, I'd get a sugar spike.

"The cat did that?" I asked, tracing my finger on her scars. I had no idea. But then, we were six years apart. I'd been too young to remember.

"Bagheera scratched me that day, and forever and until the day they died they both hated me. Catsby would wait for me by every door and bite my ankles." She laughed, but I recognized the fear she still felt when she remembered.

"They were jealous," Beli said. "Because you spent so much time with Hayden even then."

Hayden blushed and nodded. "They respected you in the end, though. Right, Jul?"

Julieta scrunched up her nose. "Did they?"

We all laughed, more to break up the tension than because it was funny. I'd never known Hayden's cats had been her enemies. That explained why she didn't like cats. But then, why did she want a kitten for Hayden? To compete for his attention? It didn't sound smart to me.

"Ah!" Beli exclaimed, startling us all, including Gigi. "I left the quesitos in the oven." She ran to the kitchen.

"So," I said eagerly, "to make sure I understood correctly: Mami said yes? Just like that? She said I can keep the kittens until they're old enough?"

Hayden petted Gigi, and Julieta smiled again. "Yes. She said you won't get to keep any of them, but that they can stay until they're old enough."

That had been exactly what I wanted, but the thought of saying goodbye to the cats dampened my mood like a cloud blocking the sun on a pool day.

"She also said that if you can't find homes, they'll have to go to the shelter, so to keep that in mind. They go on Valentine's Day and not a day later. Also, she won't be in charge of anything. It's your time to shine, sis."

I knew now the shelter wasn't the scary place of outdated movies. But I loved the kittens, and if I couldn't keep them, I wanted to be the one finding them the best homes. Now I had to figure out how to place them.

Julieta and Hayden left to go skiing with their friend Sienna, and I ate a slightly burned pastelito by the nest, mesmerized at how beautiful the kittens were. Until someone knocked on the door.

Beli went to answer, and a voice exclaimed, "You gotta be kitten me! Still not dressed for the day?"

I laughed even before I turned to see Reuben's face, reddened by the cold.

"What are you doing up so early?" I asked.

Beli ruffled his hair as he walked in. "I have a plan!" He grinned and showed me the first page in his notebook, entitled "Operation Kitten Cupid."

Chapter 6
Playing Cupid

Reuben and I plotted while the kittens slept. They would be ready to go to their fur-ever homes at eight weeks old, but the logistics would start now. Operation Kitten Cupid would help us find their future owners.

They only woke up to nurse or when their mama left them for some much-needed food and potty breaks. Every time the babies missed their mama's warm body next to them, they meowed pitifully and tried to find her, their tiny limbs jerking in fits. As soon as their cries became frantic, Gigi gobbled down her food and went back to her babies. She licked the crumbs of the kitten milk replacement powder sprinkled on the menudo Beli had prepared.

"At least someone loves my food," Beli said dramatically.

After much deliberation, we finally agreed on the most important thing—names. Going with the royal theme, we settled on John (Johnnycakes) for one of the gray kittens, Josefina (Fifi) for his twin, Meghan (Meggie) for the orange girl, Henry (Harry) for the tuxedo boy, and Maxima (Max) for the rainbow baby.

I wondered what Meera would have wanted to name them. Last year, she would have been here with us.

Reuben insisted that once we had names, the following item on the agenda was the adoption plan.

As we thought, I ate the mac and cheese I'd made myself from a box mix. To make my grandma happy, I'd put some beans in a corner of the plate, but I didn't love the spices in Puerto Rican food, and I definitely didn't like menudo.

Reuben was another story. He ate anything put in front of him, especially if the food had taken hours of preparation, like his mom's arepas or Beli's menudo. Judging by the three servings and the look of utter bliss on his face, the menudo was exceptional. I didn't know where he stored all the food he ate. He was skinny like a straw. He was tall, though, compared to me at least. Between bites, he scribbled in the notebook.

"We could stand by a corner at the roundabout with posters," Reuben said as he sipped on the kids' piña colada Beli had made him. "You know the girl who sells the fudge there earns tons of money every week?"

"I'm not interested in standing for hours, begging for someone to take them off our hands, Reuben." I had a hot chocolate for dessert in front of me. "If we do that, any person could come asking for a kitten and we'd have no way to know if they have good intentions." The babies hadn't even been born yesterday at this time, but by now, they were my heart. I had to make sure they'd be happy forever, and that their future humans really loved them unconditionally and in the way they deserved.

"We need to make it so everyone wants one. Supply and demand, remember?" I said.

Math was my weakness, but I loved how businesses worked. I started Slime Supreme because I loved playing with slime, and I loved to share it with others. But materials were expensive, so I had to charge more than that to buy supplies. Still, I couldn't keep up with the demand, so Papi had explained to me the laws of supply and demand. The more limited the goods were, the more expensive or difficult to get they became.

There were only five kittens, plus the mamacat, and I was hoping there would be more than six families who wanted them.

Reuben exchanged a look with Beli, who was sitting in a sunbeam by the window as she knitted with pink and red yarn.

"We can't make it look like we want to get rid of them," I said. "They're precious. Don't you see?"

"It would be easier, that's all I mean," Reuben said, and Beli nodded, siding with him. "Besides, *your mom* said that if the kittens don't have permanent homes by Valentine's, then they go to the shelter. Which, you know, our local shelter is a good place, but they're swamped already. They can use all the help they can get." He accentuated each word with a knock on the table. "What should we do?"

I eyed Beli. She was concentrating on counting stitches. I took my chance and whispered my idea to Reuben. "I was thinking that we could set up a contest. Kind of like the lottery we did for the most exclusive slime flavors. Only serious slimers could buy a ticket. Remember?"

Reuben shuddered, and I wasn't sure if it was because he was cold, or if my words brought back bad memories. He had reason for both. It was freezing in here, and I still had nightmares about Slime Supreme.

At first, the exclusive slime lottery had been a total success. But soon, people started complaining that the new system made them feel left out. Meera and I couldn't agree on a solution, and without consulting me, she'd posted the recipe for Caribbean Blue on our AstroSnap account. Caribbean Blue was the special formula Papi and I had created. She had no right to give it away.

The whole fifth grade took sides, mostly with Meera. They thought I was just being mean, keeping the recipes and exclusive slimes to myself for no reason. When word reached Mrs. Snow, the principal, she'd declared Slime

Supreme done forever. Meera and I had hardly spoken since. I may have been in trouble plenty of other times, but it was *Meera* who earned me my reputation. Instead of apologizing to me, she'd started crying, saying she'd wanted to include everyone.

"It will be different this time," I said, patting Reuben's hand. "We could have an application with questions to weed out people who aren't serious about having a pet, or who wouldn't be ideal candidates. In the meantime, I'll make profiles for the kittens, like in the book Mrs. Jenkins read the class last year, remember *Gaby, Lost and Found*? Then I'll match up each kitten to one of the candidates and have them meet on Valentine's Day. Or no! The day before so they can spend their first Valentine's together. What do you think?"

"Valentine's is on a Saturday this year," Reuben said. "I guess it would work." Reuben shrugged a shoulder, and I knew exactly what he wasn't saying. That given my reputation and the whole thing with Slime Supreme, not a lot of people would apply for a kitten if they knew *I* was behind the Kitten Operation.

"No one has to know I'm in charge," I said quietly. "Or that you are, for that matter, because then they'll put two and two together, and people will guess."

"It'll be hard to keep it from Meera," Reuben said. He tried to seem neutral, but every time he talked about her, he blushed to the tips of his ears. She was a topic we avoided for the sake of our friendship. I was sure he already knew about Cap, and I was grateful he'd come to help me when she probably needed just as much support. But Meera had a lot of friends. I only had Reuben.

Unlike everyone else in our grade, Reuben had refused to take sides, staying friends with both of us. I pretended it didn't hurt that he didn't completely side with me, but until now, his split loyalty hadn't been a problem.

Meera and I had known each other most of our lives, being neighbors and all. Then we met Reuben at resource class, where Meera and I both got the extra help we needed for math. Meera because of her dyslexia, and me for dyscalculia, two faces of the same coin. My dyscalculia was why I had a hard time understanding numbers, just like Meera mixed up letters and words.

Reuben had ADHD, but not the disruptive kind. He just traveled in his mind and missed complete lessons if he wasn't careful.

"Meera can't know," I said, and it sounded like a warning. "If she finds out, then the whole school will know the truth, and the kittens will end up in the shelter. Like you said, the shelter needs all the help it can get, and we can help. Besides, we can be more detailed with the application process."

Reuben's eyes widened. "More extra, you mean."

I sighed, frustrated.

Reuben patted my hand and said, "You make it sound like it will be a *cat*astrophe if *you* don't find the kittens homes."

"It *will* be, Reuben. I'm serious," I said. "What if the kittens go to homes where they're not treated the absolute best? I know there's a perfect home out there for each of these little cuties. And if you betray me and the kittens go to less than ideal homes because you can't keep the secret from Meera . . . then I guess you're not a real friend after all. You don't have to help me. I understand."

There was a brief pause, and who knew what was going on in his mind, but I prayed silently that he wouldn't leave, that he'd choose me instead of Meera for once.

Finally, when my eyes had startled prickling, he nodded and said, "I won't say anything. I promise."

"Good," I said, hoping my voice sounded cool as mama-cat's nose and not shaky with relief like I actually felt. "The plan is this, then: I'll study the applicants and watch them closely before making a decision. When people don't really talk to you, you have the chance to observe them. I'll be able to match the kittens to the kids who deserve them."

"So, we make a *cat*-alog, and a people-log," Reuben said, taking notes. He still had two bright splotches in his cheeks.

"Exactly," I said, not falling for his cheesiness this time, but appreciating it all the same. "The pairings have to be perfect so everyone wins."

Reuben leaned toward me with his forearms resting on the table. "But how do we spread the word if you don't want to put up posters? You don't have access to your Astro account yet, do you?"

I shook my head sadly. AstroSnap was the school platform for social media communications. The PTA had come up with it to keep students off sites parents couldn't control. My account got locked when Slime Supreme collapsed. After all, I did the main marketing through AstroSnap. I tried to convince the principal that Astro hadn't been the problem. That it was all Meera's fault for posting the recipe there. But without listening to my reasons, Mami and Principal Snow agreed that it was best if I canceled my Astro, which ended my social life.

Which didn't mean I didn't keep up with the school through a loophole Mami hadn't known about. I'd just created a Fake Astro, a FAstro. Everyone had one.

"I don't have an Astro . . ." I said, adding a pause for suspense. "But there's my FAstro."

Reuben smiled slyly. "I knew it! You've been lurking the whole time? What's your username?"

Now it was my turn to shrug only one shoulder. The less he knew, the better. "It's not important. Tonight, I'll change it to Operation Kitten, or . . . wait!" I exclaimed, my mind lighting up with an idea. "What about Operation Kitten Cupid. OKC for short."

Reuben raised an eyebrow. "Oklahoma City? Like the Thunder?"

"Yikes, no, then . . . What about Kitten Cupid?"

"Purrfect!" he said.

"I'll post a link to the survey-slash-application, and then I'll update with pictures and videos of the kittens. That way we'll keep the interest going until before Valentine's and spread the word on the importance of volunteering and fostering, and even spaying and neutering pets. That way, the message will help other kittens besides mine."

Reuben thought, tapping a pen to his chin. He must have not found a flaw in the plan because he finally nodded. "I'll help you write up the application and then read the entries with you. How about that?"

I loved the idea.

Then he scrunched up his nose and asked, "We're making a profile for the mom too, right? A total of six cats to find homes for." He stuck his tongue out as he jotted in his notebook.

Something wild jumped in my heart, just like when the mamacat had made herself bigger and fiercer when she was protecting her babies. "Not the mama . . . I'm going to keep Gigi," I said, and Reuben looked at me as if I were speaking in pig latin. "If no one claims her, I'm going to keep her."

Reuben chewed at the end of his pencil. "And . . . your mom will let you?"

If I asked my mom now, she'd say no. And really, I had no idea what mess I was getting myself into wanting to keep Gigi, but I couldn't imagine having her go through the whole process of finding a new family. She'd chosen *me* to protect her. She'd found me. I shrugged.

"Well, if you say so . . . That's five kitten profiles, then."

"Yes, and to spread the word, I'll need *you* to pretend you want a kitten. People follow your advice, basketball team captain." I playfully tapped his arms, which looked puny but were actually three-point-shot-launching machines.

The spark in Reuben's eye flickered and then died.

"What?" I asked, worried about the change in his expression. "It's not like you'll have to get one, you know?"

He hesitated, like he didn't know how to tell me something, when his phone went off. He looked down at the screen and said, "My mom's here. Time to start the Christmas festivities now that I'm not sick anymore."

Just then, we coughed in unison, and we laughed, but deep down, I was disappointed to miss some Christmas fun.

"You can go. It's not a big deal," I said. "Stay healthy because I'll need you on that first day of school. And remember, not a word to Meera."

Reuben made the gesture of zipping up his lips and throwing away the key. A car honked outside, and he headed to the front door. Before he left, though, he turned around and said, "Don't forget to put the letter *M* in the freezer."

For a second, I thought he was talking about Meera or some obscure holiday tradition I'd forgotten about, like lighting Advent candles or moving the donkey closer to the Nativity.

"Put the *M* in the freezer?" I asked.

"For the kittens!" His smile was so cheesy he could hardly talk. "The *M* turns the ice into *mice*." There was a pause and then he said, "Get it?"

The memory of his laughter, and the excitement of surprising people with a kitten on Valentine's Day, kept me going through the day.

It helped me through the following ten days actually, the whole winter break and the holidays, empty of Papi, but full of kittens and purrs. Ten days of newborn kittens.

Every time Papi called, I was conveniently busy with the cats or asleep, recovering from the nighttime feedings.

But on the day before school, I woke up with butterflies in my stomach. It was the most pet-acular feeling to post the first Kitten Cupid video sequence made up of photos of the kittens' first days.

The caption read:

Andromeda Elementary, find your purrfect Valentine. After all, nothing says love like a purring kitten in your arms.

Maybe it was the fuzzy feelings in my heart watching the video over and over as the views rose, but I gave in to an impulse and sent the video to my dad too.

You would love them, I wrote.

My fingers hovered over the keyboard, waiting for my heart to dictate the next words, but I didn't know how to turn my feelings into sentences. After all, I wasn't like favorita Julieta, who always knew the perfect thing to say.

Maybe a drawing would be best. I'd draw a tornado of grays and blacks, and a tiny splash of color in a corner, representing Reuben and my cats. But I couldn't make my dad sad about me, thousands of miles away. He had more important things to do than worry about my feelings. Things like staying alive.

No. If I sent him a message telling him I was so sad, he'd

tell Mami, and then she'd be upset I wasn't trying to be happy. The splash of color in my life was all Papi would get to see for now. He could guess about the whirlwind in my heart.

Besides, I had many things to work through, like how to deal with the avalanche of applications. I was positive that when word spread about the kittens, everyone would want one. And maybe when at the end I revealed it was me behind the whole thing, people would realize how unfairly they'd treated me. I wasn't the mean, selfish girl who'd made Meera cry and didn't want to share the slime recipes. No one had made the effort to understand that not everyone cries when they have a broken heart. The recipe was something special I shared with my dad, and Meera had taken it away from me.

But I would show them. Maybe, for even just a day, I could be everyone's favorite.

For the first time in sixth grade, I was excited to go to school the next day.

Chapter 7
Drop the 'Tude

The alarm went off, and a horrible heaviness pressed down on my chest.

"No, no," I whispered. I didn't want to start the second half of sixth grade like I'd started the first half, back in September. That day, I'd woken up with crushing anxiety over how people would treat me after the fight with Meera and the failure of Slime Supreme.

Now I tried to push all the darkness to the corner of my soul until I could deal with it at night when no one could see me. I pictured the perfect softness and plumpness of Johnnycakes's paws, the dainty valentine of Fifi's nose. Gigi's purring when she bathed the babies, and the way Max's tiny tummy rose gently while she slept. But the heaviness wouldn't go away, and when I took a deep breath, the heaviness started . . . rumbling . . . ?

No, it was purring!

I opened my eyes to see Gigi sitting on my chest.

I laughed and Gigi's ears twitched. She dipped her head down and licked my face with her scratchy tongue.

"Good morning, Queen Georgiana," I said in a croaky voice, wiping my face with the back of my hand so I wouldn't hurt her feelings. But I knew too much of what she cleaned with that picker-upper tongue.

In response, she meowed and jumped off the bed. She looked over her shoulder, and I understood she wanted me to follow her. She walked toward the laundry room with the grace of a true queen.

"Okay, okay," I said, untangling myself from my heavy antianxiety blanket and stumbling in the dark after her. By now, she knew I'd follow her to the ends of the world, and I thanked my lucky stars that no one had called from the vet claiming her.

The microwave clock said it was only 5:55 a.m. After

days of routine, was Gigi suddenly afraid I'd forget to feed Max at 6:00? Or worse, had something happened to one of the babies? The leftover drowsiness fled like a spooked bird.

I ran to check on the nest. The kittens were sleeping, but Meggie, the orange tabby girl, was squirming and chirping, missing her mama already. Gigi started wolfing down her food without even chewing. She meowed again over her shoulder. She seemed to be telling me something, but I couldn't understand what.

And then I saw it. I saw her.

Max's eyes were open! She was following my every move, and when I stretched out my hand to pick her up, she meowed softly.

"Good morning," I whispered, and kissed her tiny velvety black nose.

The other kittens meowed too, either responding to my voice or crying because they missed their mama. I inspected each one of them, and all of their eyes were open. Fifi's just barely, but she was trying to unglue her eyelids, as if she couldn't wait to see the whole wide world. Reuben had emailed me a chart that said their eyes would open between nine and twelve days, and this was technically day twelve. The babies had been born premature, so it was natural they were on the slower end. One thing they all had down was the purring. They'd been little rumbling love engines since day one.

Outside the window, the snow sparkled like diamonds, and a silver sliver of moon shone in a parting of the dark clouds. It wasn't a star to make a wish on, but I sent a kiss and a hug, hoping it would bounce on the moon and then back to Earth. I hoped my love would reach my dad, wherever he was.

Although there was that sticky sadness and its friend anxiety in the bottom of the ocean of my emotions, on the top of my heart the waves were mostly happy. With my cats, I didn't have to pretend. And when I was sad, they just waited for me to breathe it out.

"What are you doing up already?" Mami asked, startling me. She'd spoken softly, but I realized she'd been watching me watching the moon and mumbling silly things to it. I got embarrassed.

The good feelings evaporated so quickly even I was surprised when I exclaimed, "What time does a person have to get up to get some quiet time in this house?"

Mami's eyes hardened as she shook her head and headed to the kitchen to get a cup of coffee.

"Since you're up, get ready for school. Stop fussing over the kittens. They must be celebrating you'll be gone for hours so they can sleep in peace."

"Yes, I understand the feeling. I always celebrate when you're gone all day and I have to be home by myself." The sarcasm turned my words into a hiss. I imagined inside I looked like an angry cat. Even Gigi sent me a disapproving look.

Seeing my mom's expression, I wished I could turn back time and not say such hurtful words. I hadn't intended for the morning to start this way. Why was it so hard to at least *appear* to be happy? Instead, my sadness leaked out as anger. Pretending to be happy was technically a way of lying, but no adults, especially my mom, had a problem with it. This attitude was what got me in trouble every time, but I didn't know how to change.

Before I could apologize and then turn the conversation to a happy topic, like the babies opening their eyes, Mami said, "Just so you know, Meera and Bodhi are going to ride to school with us for the next couple of weeks."

I choked on my good intentions. "They what?" I had no problems with Bodhi. He was adorable. But Meera?

Mami closed her eyes in that way that meant she was praying for patience. "Natalia, take a breath and drop that attitude."

"What attitude? Mami, after what happened with Meera, you think I'm going to share a ride with her?"

Beli peeked her head out of her door, and when she saw Mami and me arguing, she went back into Julieta's room. The whispers and muffled laughter between them didn't make me feel any better.

"You're welcome to walk to school, then," Mami said. "When Vidya asked me the favor late last night, I couldn't say no."

"I'll walk, then," I said.

I saw the lightning in Mami's eyes when she was about to reply. Thunder would follow, and I braced myself for it. Suddenly, Gigi went over to my mom and rubbed her head on Mami's leg. The tension between us broke, a bubble of anger popped by a purr and a headbutt.

Mami sighed and in a calmer voice asked, "Haven't you noticed that Brian has cleared our sidewalk every day it has snowed because Papi is out of town? The least I can do is drive the kids. In spite of the fight between you two, Meera is a nice girl. And Bodhi? What has that child done to you?"

Bodhi was an angel boy. I had nothing against him. And it had been kind of Meera's dad to think of us. But why did that mean I had to put myself at Meera's mercy? My mom had no clue of how much worse she was making me feel.

Why couldn't she take my side for once? Did she think forcing me in the same car with Meera was being nice to me, her own daughter?

"Remember that lo cortés no quita lo valiente, Natalia. Just because I like the Rogerses, it doesn't mean I don't love you, you know?"

With that, the discussion was over. How was I supposed to counter her argument that being polite didn't take away from being brave? Being polite had only made me look weak, and now I had to put up with Meera on the ride to school every day for who knew how long. Also, what if Bodhi hated me too?

But Mami didn't give me the chance to change her mind. Soon, the family went into back-to-school mode.

Julieta left with Hayden, and then the clock struck seven thirty, which meant I had to leave too. On my way out the door, Beli kissed me on the cheek and said, "The babies will be safe with me."

Beli's words were the only reason I could make myself leave the kittens. What would I do when she was gone?

When Meera got into the car next to me, I had the impulse to open the door and run all the way to school, or better yet, back home. We looked at each other for just a moment before I turned to look out the window. Bodhi clicked his seat belt and sat in silence as my mom gushed at Meera's every word and fake smile.

Making an effort to tune them out, I thought of how Gigi had trusted me enough to show me her babies opening their eyes. What would it be like to see the world for the first time?

I'd always thought trees were naked in the winter, but now I noticed the sparkle in them that made them look as if they were dressed in sequins and crystals. If the kittens looked out the window with me, they'd see how bright and blue the sky looked after the snow. They'd also see how Meera smirked at me when Mami wasn't looking, and how she twisted the charm of a paw print in her bracelet. I wondered if it represented Captain America for her, and if she missed him.

"I heard Cap passed away," Mami said, her thoughts

obviously aligned with mine. "He had a good life with your family, though."

Bodhi gave out a deep sigh of sadness, and Meera's smile drooped. This time, her expression seemed genuine instead of a show for the adults. "He got really sick, and we had to put him to sleep. I miss him so much" was all she said, and then she looked out the window.

The silence was unbearable, and I was about to say I was sorry for her loss when Mami added, "Dogs are the best companions in life. Maybe you can get another one soon?"

I internally rolled my eyes, and even without seeing Meera's face, I knew she was annoyed by Mami's comment.

Meera and I had always wondered why people said that when someone lost a pet. Even if another one came to the family and brought happiness and love, nothing and no one could replace the one that had just died or gone away. We knew because, before her family got Cap, Meera had a lion-head bunny named Periwinkle. Even Captain America, the best dog ever, couldn't *replace* Mr. Peri. And now no pet would ever truly replace Cap.

Last year, Meera and I would have shared an understanding look, like those I'd seen between Beli and Mami, or Julieta and Mami. But now the ride continued in silence until Bodhi said, "Actually, it's my turn to choose a pet, and I want a cat."

My heart went into panic mode.

"There he goes again," Meera said, patting her brother's hand. "He didn't get a cat for Christmas and now he's pretending he's a cat. He calls himself Niño Gato," she explained to Mom, acting like I wasn't even there.

"Is that right?" Mami asked, looking at Bodhi through the rearview mirror.

"Meow, meow" was his reply.

Meera and Mami laughed, but pins and needles of nerves stabbed the skin of my whole body. Fearing Mami would say something about the kittens and blow my cover with Meera, I reached over and patted her shoulder. She winked at me through the mirror, and I had no other choice but to trust that she'd keep the kitten business secret.

When we finally arrived at school, my whole body hurt

from holding the tension. Meera didn't seem to notice, though. She smiled brightly at my mom. "Thanks, Gina," she said. I hated that she called my mom by her first name as if our families were still friends with each other. "See you later." She didn't even look in my direction. It was like I didn't even exist.

She helped her little brother out of the car, and her friends called out when they saw her. They ran to hug her, phones in hands.

But no one waited for me, and before jumping into the torture of sixth grade, I took a deep breath.

"Have a great day," Mami said in the singsongy voice she reserved for asking impossible things. But since she hadn't revealed my secret, I was careful not to slam the door on my way out.

Chapter 8
Andromeda's Sweetie

As I waited for the bell to ring, I shivered next to the flag pole. But the cold wasn't the worst part.

Around me, exclamations of happiness exploded every few seconds as friends reunited after the break. Meera and her friends huddled around a phone, looking at something that had them all smiling. Someone knocked into my shoulder—Jojo and her twin sister, Sam, as they ran to join the other girls. Sam kept going without a look in my direction, not even to apologize, but Jojo waved at me when she made sure her sister wouldn't see. They didn't even look like twins. Jojo was shorter and dressed in a pastel sweater and a giant bow on her head. Sam's jeans were always ripped, the bottoms of her tennis shoes were full of doodles, and a pink stripe peeked through her hair.

I wondered if Principal Snow would write her up for breaking the dress code that forbid *unnatural hair colors*, but I doubted it. Sam was one of the principal's favorite students, maybe because she was on student council, maybe because she always smiled at all the teachers. I didn't know.

The twins had been two of Slime Supreme's most loyal customers, and when I was forced to close operations, they took out their frustration on me. I still wanted to be selling them Cotton Candy Blue and Pineapple Sublime, but they never even listened to my explanations. The twins still talked to Meera and fought for her attention, though, as if the whole thing hadn't been her fault.

Meera must have been telling them about Cap because Sam patted her shoulder, and Jojo had a face like she might burst into tears at any second. Lilah, a redheaded girl who'd always invited me to her birthday parties, at least until last year, glanced at me and said something that made the others crack a smile. Meera added something else, and this time the smiles turned into full belly laughter.

Were they laughing at me? At something my mom had said in the car?

Soon enough, Valentine's Day would come. And when that happened, when everyone discovered I was the person giving out the kittens, how would the rest of the sixth grade react?

I looked around for a miracle. Maybe Reuben would be early for once, but there was no trace of his freckly face.

Finally, the first bell rang, and the younger kids ran to line up by their door.

"Bienvenidos, niños," Mrs. Ruiz, Bodhi's first-grade Spanish immersion teacher, called.

My class was heading in after the first graders, and I stood aside to let everyone enter ahead of me. Behind me, Meera was still talking to her friends.

"Why didn't he get a kitty?" Lilah asked.

"We couldn't find one, actually," Meera said. "In the newspaper classified section, all the cats were either expensive breeds like Siamese or the hairless type, or too old to be rehomed. He wants a kitten to grow up with, and my dad insists it has to be a rescue."

Susan the nurse had been right. Everyone wanted a baby. Once an animal grew out of the cute kitten phase, all big eyes and milky breath, then their chances for real love nose-dived. I imagined Gigi in a shelter, waiting and waiting, never loved just because she'd dared to grow up. My heart clenched, the opposite of a purr.

No, she'd stay with me forever. I had to convince my mom somehow.

I turned around just in time to see Lilah's face light up. "But did you see that ad for the cutest kittens on the Astro feed? What good timing!"

I almost stumbled as we stepped into the building. Meera didn't notice that I was eavesdropping as she took off her chunky knitted white hat, releasing a mass of gorgeous brown hair that belonged in a shampoo commercial. The smell of the argan oil her mom sprayed on her head before brushing it mixed with the scent of pencil shavings, industrial floor cleaner, and bacon from breakfast at the school cafeteria.

"Really? I have to check! It would work just perfectly if I can get one for Bodhi," she said.

"I'm going to apply for one when the application link is up," Lilah added, and Jojo listened with an interested expression on her face.

My breath caught in my throat when I reached the door of my classroom and Jojo said, "I wonder who's managing Kitten Cupid? The quality of the graphics was kind of wonky, but the kittens are adorable, even the mom."

I stood frozen while they walked into their classroom. The second bell rang, prodding me into action. Of course Lilah knew about the kittens already—isn't that what I'd wanted? In a daze, I headed to my class and, for the next hour, pretended to work at math. Honestly, my mind was buzzing with excitement that Andromeda Elementary already knew about the kittens, *even* if the quality of my posts wasn't Slime Supreme level.

When Mrs. Thomas, my teacher, started walking around the classroom, I hurried to fill in answers just so she'd believe I'd been busy. She stopped by my desk, and when she looked at my paper, she clicked her tongue.

I looked up and smiled at her, trying to charm her with my personality now that my smarts were failing me. The smile she returned didn't look amused at all.

"I know it's hard to come back to school after the break," she said. "And I know these exercises are hard for you, but you have to try, Natalia."

My cheeks flamed when the people around me snickered. I had a mild headache just looking at the tricky fractions, but I picked up my pencil again so Mrs. Thomas would turn her disappointed attention on someone else. My resource teacher, Mr. Warthon, would help me finish the math assignment.

In the back of the room, Lilah and Sam whispered behind their hands and giggled, looking at me. Lilah had never made fun of me for going to resource before, but in the fall I'd heard her snickering about it. I tried to pretend I didn't care about the girls, but it was hard not to be bitter. Last year, I'd been one of them.

The thoughts blaring in my mind did nothing but make

my headache worse. I longed for some slime to knead, or the purring of a kitten next to my heart, to calm me. But Principal Snow had banned slime from the school because of me, and I was pretty sure she wouldn't agree to comfort kittens either.

By the time the recess bell rang, I was ready to bolt out of the room to find Reuben. But as I was putting my things away, Mrs. Thomas called me over. "Natalia, let's work on the social studies assignments you missed when you were sick before the break."

"Ay, no!" I exclaimed. When I realized I'd just talked back to the teacher, I clapped a hand over my mouth. "I'm sorry," I said. "Can I take them home instead? I just need some fresh air now."

Mrs. Thomas wasn't impressed with my outburst. She shook her head and moved a chair next to hers at the big desk. "It won't take you too long," she said.

I pressed my lips to stop any more inappropriate words from coming out of my mouth, but I could do nothing to stop the tears that sprang to my eyes. I quickly blinked them away. The teacher couldn't see me cry. I plopped on the chair, and huffing, I grabbed the pencil and started filling out the map of ancient Italy with the names of mountains. Next time I time-traveled to the birth of Rome, all this knowledge would be very useful in case Romulus and Remus asked for directions.

It wasn't until I was halfway done that I looked up from my own misery long enough to see that Jojo had stayed behind too. She was gazing out the window, clearly struggling with her own worksheet. When she felt my eyes on her, Jojo looked at me and smiled. Now I wondered if Lilah and Sam had been laughing at me or at Jojo.

I hurried to finish my assignment, hoping to catch at least a minute of recess, but too soon the bell rang.

As we slouched back to our regular seats, Jojo put a hand in her pocket and took out a Haribo gummy bears mini pack. She extended it in my direction. "For you," she said.

Gummy bears were my favorite. "Thank you," I said, but Jojo had already turned around to get to work.

The class quickly filed into the room, their cheeks rosy from running in the snow. Under the cover of the desk, I opened the plastic baggie and ate a gummy bear. Sour strawberry flavor exploded on my tongue, and I smiled at Jojo over my shoulder. Sam saw me and muttered something at Jojo, who quickly looked away.

A sudden burst of appreciation for my sister warmed my heart. Julieta was the favorite daughter, but she never left me to fend for myself.

The teacher started going over the new social studies material—current events—but I got distracted thinking of something nice I could do for Jojo to cheer her up. She'd seemed interested when the girls had been talking about the kittens. If she decided to apply for one, I'd consider her, even if her sister was mean.

Mrs. Thomas plopped an issue of the *Andromeda Herald*, the local newspaper, on my desk. It was from mid-December.

Since I hadn't been paying attention and had no idea what the assignment was, I looked around to get a clue. Everyone was flipping newspaper pages. Following the crowd, I opened my copy to a random page.

When my eyes landed on a full-page, full-color ad of a cat that looked uncannily like Gigi, I gasped.

The note below it read:

Wanted. Our cat, Sweetie, went missing and we're moving out of state next week. We need to find her now. Please call us!

This couldn't be true. I studied the cat's face, trying to find proof it wasn't who I thought it was, but all the markings were the same. Even the dainty white paws that looked like velvet shoes were identical to the cat nursing her babies in my house right now.

My queen Georgiana, my Gigi, had a family. They'd been looking for her weeks ago when she went missing.

While I was having a crisis, Mrs. Thomas gave instructions to the whole class. "Choose a news headline and write an article about how it relates to our community." There was a wave of murmuring around the class.

Ignoring the protests, Mrs. Thomas added, "Now, the topic you choose has to be an issue you're passionate about and that can create awareness for something others might not even know about."

I doubted there was anything I'd be passionate enough about in the whole newspaper. The picture of Gigi had been the least welcome thing in my morning, and there had been many things competing for the honor. At least I wasn't the only one who didn't understand the instructions.

"Can you give us an example, Mrs. Thomas?" Lilah asked. I was so grateful she'd been brave enough to ask.

Mrs. Thomas smiled, obviously having fun with this assignment. She grabbed Lincoln's paper and browsed through the pages.

"Here!" she said, showing the class a page full of colorful ads. "There's an ad for a new boutique on Center Street. You can write about your favorite businesses downtown. Here's a profile on the new vet, Dr. Michael Kay. You can write about the services a vet provides to the community, or to your own pets."

The class rumbled, confused.

Mrs. Thomas continued, "There's a small piece about the rodeo coming this summer. You could research the rodeos in the area, or the different events, or spotlight rodeo champions and queens in the last couple years. In short, you could take this topic in any direction you want. This way, we'll make current events relevant to you. It will also be good practice for seventh grade, when you'll have to write research papers. Have fun with it, class! It's due in two weeks."

Excited voices filled the room, but even though I flipped through the pages of the newspaper I'd gotten, all I could think about was the wanted ad for Gigi. Or Sweetie, actually. What kind of name was that for a queen?

After quiet reading time and science, I was ready for a break. When the lunch bell rang, I quickly tried to sneak out of the room before Mrs. Thomas made me stay again, but she was waiting at the door for me.

I must have made a face because she said, "Don't look so worried, Natalia. I was only going to ask if you would prefer coming to school a little earlier to do your work." She paused, and when she realized I didn't understand what she was saying, she added, "That way you won't miss any recess. I saw you haven't been too happy all morning."

I would've mentioned how I wasn't happy that she was stopping me from meeting Reuben at lunch, but I remembered my manners and said, "Come to school early? For language arts too?"

"I know it doesn't sound fun, but a few other kids come early for tutoring, and I'd be happy to add you to our little group."

I thought quickly. This was a perfect opportunity to get out of riding with Meera in the mornings. Before I could consider my actions, I said, "Okay. I'll be here early."

Mrs. Thomas made a note on her clipboard, and then said, "We meet half an hour before the bell. Be on time."

Behind Mrs. Thomas, Reuben made eyes for me to join him on the way to lunch. I smiled at my teacher and walked quickly to join my friend.

At lunch, Reuben took a big bite of the Cuban sandwich Beli had made me bring for him before he whispered, "Everyone in class was talking about the kittens. We need to get that link up soon so people can start applying."

Meera was sitting at the Spanish immersion kids' table, sending looks at Reuben. Maybe the fact that he was friends with both of us was hard for her too.

Reuben waved at Meera, and she smiled briefly at him but continued eating with her other friends. Reuben's face fell a little. I didn't know how to feel when I noticed a little coldness between them.

"Who's everyone, and what did they really say?" I asked.

"When I say everyone, I mean everyone," Reuben said, and took a swig of apple juice. "They said the graphics are blurry, though."

I wished Meera's slime videos hadn't set the bar so high. If the school had been used to wonky graphics to start with, I wouldn't have had to worry about how clunky mine were.

"Come over to my house today after your practice," I said to Reuben. "There will be more of those Cubanos waiting for you. And I have something to tell you." I wished I could tell him now about the ad for Gigi/Sweetie, which was eating out a hole in my heart, but it was too complicated to go over everything when Reuben obviously wanted to run to his other friends.

"I can't wait to see those kittens! Especially mine."

I laughed when he wiggled his eyebrows. He was such a clown.

He swallowed the last bite of the sandwich and whispered, "I'll bring sample applications from pet shelters. You make sure we have a clear photo of each kitten and a little bio to go with it."

"Okay. One other thing—let's not talk about this at resource. Meera will hear, and you know . . ."

"Paw-sitive?" he asked, his eyes glinting with worry. "I'll be careful."

"I know. But just in case," I said.

He shrugged, and with these instructions, he left to join some of the other boys in the school yard. I could see through the window as they built an igloo. Even though it was more mud and grass than snow, it still looked kind of fun. I wished Reuben would invite me over, but there were no other girls in their group. Besides, I wasn't looking forward to suffering through the rest of school with sopping wet socks.

At the popular kids table, Meera finished her lunch on her own, and when we made eye contact, her cheeks flushed bright red and we both quickly looked away.

Chapter 9
So Extra

"Gigi!" I called when I opened the front door.

Gigi ran to meet me, and I knelt down for her to give me the headbutt that meant she loved me. The stress I carried on my shoulders all the way home, walking behind Meera, her brother, and her friends, melted like the old snow on the sidewalk under the afternoon sun.

"I missed you so much!" I said, thrilled that she was letting me hug her.

A choir of tiny meows called her back to the nest in the laundry room, and after a slow blink that I liked to think meant she'd missed me too, she broke free of my arms and sauntered back to her babies.

Beli was standing in the kitchen, looking at me. "Ay, qué amores!" She placed a plate of empanadillas on the table.

I went over to her and gave her a hug. She smelled of sugar and her Avon perfume, Sweet Honesty, which is probably what made me blurt out what had been gnawing at my heart all day long. "You won't believe what I discovered," I said. "Gigi's real name is Sweetie, and she had a family, and—" My voice broke. It was just too much for all the feelings to come out in order.

Beli sat on a chair and, now that we were at eye level, said, "Tell me from the beginning."

I took out the newspaper from my backpack and opened it to the lost cat ad. She studied the picture for long seconds, her eyes scanning the whole page, her lips reading over the words. She stood up with paper in hand as she walked to the laundry room. In the pause that followed, I quickly washed my hands and grabbed an empanadilla that was still warm and fragrant. Once Reuben arrived, I wouldn't have the chance to even taste one. I bit down on the slightly sweet dough, and the tangy flavors of cheese and guayaba burst on my tongue. In my catalog of what love feels like, a purring kitten and the taste of Beli's cooking were right next to each other at the top of my list.

Finally, Beli came back to the kitchen, pressing her lips. "Sí, it's the same gata."

I plopped into a chair. "And now?"

Beli took her phone out of her pocket and said, "Now we call them to iron everything out. Let's get this out of the way."

One time, visiting Tío Mako in Puerto Rico, I got a big sliver in my foot when I'd stepped on the fallen branches of a lime tree. I'd hopped on one foot to Beli, wailing like a siren. Her response had been similar: to yank it out without drama before I had time to be afraid.

Now she dialed the number, and after two rings and a round of loud heart drumming, a woman's voice answered. I stood right next to Beli so I could listen through the phone. "Hello?" the woman said.

Beli winked at me and said, "Hello, my name is Isabel

Reyes, and I'm calling about the lost cat ad in the paper from . . ." She checked the date on the paper. "December."

The woman sighed, and so many feelings crowded in that sound. "Did you find Sweetie?"

My cheeks burned with anticipation.

"My granddaughter Natalia found her, and she's been taking care of her and the babies."

"The babies?" the woman exclaimed. "Oh, my goodness! Kittens? I . . . I'm not sure it's the same cat, then."

Beli looked at me, a question in her eyes. She offered me the phone, and after hesitating for half a second, I took it. She was right. I had to get this out of the way before I made things more complicated. What if they wanted the kittens after all and I'd already promised them to people?

"Hello," I said, my voice scratchy and nervous. "I found your cat a couple weeks ago."

Without embellishing things much, I told her the whole story of the night I'd found Gigi and her babies, right up to today when I'd seen the ad in the paper at school.

Finally, she said, "We moved to Canada the week

after she went missing . . . We didn't know she was expecting kittens, and now we can't come get her back. I'm so sad."

In the silence that followed, I understood that I'd been in the right place at the right time. Maybe Gigi had sensed that she couldn't travel with her family in her state and had tried to find help. She'd found me.

"Well, it sounds like she's safe with you and your family. Thank you so much for that. She's been a great kitten . . . I'm sad and embarrassed to say we weren't the best pet owners. Will you be able to keep her?"

In that moment Mami arrived, looking tired from work, but smiling at the sight of Beli's empanadillas. Beli stood up and gave Mami a hug and whispered the news to her. I watched my mom's face and saw the exact moment she made a decision about Gigi.

"Just a second," I said on the phone, and pressed the mute button.

"Ay, Nati," Mami said, sitting next to me. "I know what you're going to ask." In that moment, Gigi jumped on

Mami's lap and pressed her head against Mami's heart. I wished I knew what her heart was saying.

"Mami, she doesn't have a home and the owners can't take her back." I fought to make my voice steady and calm, but it was hard. "There's lots of interest in the kittens, but no one wants a grown cat. And look at her!"

Gigi meowed, and Mami's eyes softened. She petted Gigi's head, and the cat closed her eyes. Finally, after a few seconds that stretched on forever, Mami said, "Okay." I had to make an effort not to squeal for joy. "But I will say this, you can only keep one of the cats. You and Max are very attached. I've seen your face when you feed her in the mornings and nights with that tiny bottle. But we can't keep both."

I'd gotten what I'd wanted: Gigi. Why did the victory taste so bittersweet in my mouth, then? But I'd face that challenge later. If I didn't find a perfect home for Max, I'd convince Mami to let me keep her somehow. I'd enlist Papi in my efforts if it was necessary.

The woman, Gigi's first human, waited for me on the

other side of the line. I unmuted the phone and said, "Sorry I had you waiting, but my mom just arrived. She said we can keep her."

"What other choice did I have?" Mami muttered as Gigi rubbed her nose against my mom's. Mami could pretend all she wanted, but anyone could see she was as much in love with Gigi as anyone else.

"Oh, that's wonderful!" the woman exclaimed. "Now I can sleep in peace knowing she's happy with a kid who'll love and protect her. She was happy with me and my boyfriend, but she always followed children around like she couldn't get enough of them. I'm glad she found you."

"I named her Queen Georgiana, Gigi. I hope you don't mind."

"Of course not! I think Gigi is a perfect name. I have to go now, but thanks for calling me, Natalia. And I hope that because of your kindness you get a lot of blessings."

After I hung up, I looked up at Mami and, making jazz hands, said, "Congrats! We have a cat now!"

Mami shook her head, placing Gigi tenderly on the floor.

"Thank you, and now please, I'm going to finish a commission. Miss Cat Protector, make sure you find homes for *all* the other cats in the laundry room."

"Ay, Gina!" Beli said. "She's just like you when you found Flashy the rooster, remember?"

Mami sent Beli a look she usually reserved for me. "Mami, whose side are you on?"

Beli laughed. "I'm on the side of love."

Someone knocked on the door, and I ran to get it while saying, "Beli, you have to tell me that story."

"Mami!" my mom called, but her voice didn't sound upset at all. "Don't make things worse!"

I opened the door. It was Reuben.

"You look happier than a cat with a paw in a fish tank!" he said, beelining for the table and, more accurately, Beli's empanadillas.

"There's my funny amigo!" Beli said, ruffling Reuben's light brown hair.

"It's only funny if people laugh," I said, shaking my head.

"Ha ha!" He pretended to laugh as he placed a binder on

the table. "I have one hour before my basketball practice, so let's get to work!"

With an empanadilla in his mouth and another in his hand, he headed to the laundry room and came back with the silver twins: Johnnycakes and Fifi.

"I thought you said you only have an hour and to get to work. What are you doing?"

"Socializing them is work. And no, you can't be the only person they socialize with." He held the babies to his face and said, "They opened their eyes! Finally. Look how blue they are! Here." He pushed the binder in my direction. "These are different versions of the interviews pet shelters use. Choose the best questions and we can post them tonight."

Gigi came back to the kitchen, and when she spotted her babies, she jumped on Reuben's lap, took Fifi by the scruff of her neck, and walked back to the laundry with the baby in her mouth. Not before she sent Reuben a look that meant, *I'll be back for my other baby, human.*

Reuben and I started laughing.

"That was amazing!" Reuben said. "Let's go sit by the nest, then."

I followed him to the laundry room, and we sprawled all the papers on the ground. While Reuben devoured the empanadillas, he played with the babies, swinging a string over their heads like a mobile.

Gigi followed our every move, but when Reuben picked up Johnnycakes, she didn't take him back. In the meantime, I went over the list of questions.

"Keep the application one page," Reuben said, petting Gigi's head. "It'll be easier for people to answer."

"Right," I said, chewing the top of my pencil. In the end, I came up with the following kitten app:

1. Personal information (name, phone, address):

2. Name, age, and species of all members of your household, including yourself and other pets:

3. Do you have any animals? Have you had any in the past? If they're no longer with you, share what happened:

4. If you currently have pets, please describe their personality:

5. What would a usual day be like for the cat in your home?

6. Why are you interested in adopting a kitten at this time?

7. Will you be the primary caregiver for the kitten?

   ☐ Yes, I am applying for myself.

   ☐ No, I am applying for someone else.

8. Is there a specific kitten/s you are interested in? (Kitten Cupid will take into consideration your preference, but we can't make any guarantees that you'll get your first pick.)

9. The cat will be:

   ☐ Indoor only

   ☐ Outdoor only

   ☐ Indoor/Outdoor

10. What will you do if you can't keep the cat?

11. Extra comments:

12. Do you agree to the $25 fee?

13. Optional: AstroSnap username:

"What do you think?" I asked Reuben, and read him the questions aloud because he was lying on the floor with all the kittens on top of him.

"I think your application is stricter than the application to move into a new student apartment," said Julieta peeking into the laundry room.

"Or join the FBI," added Hayden.

"What's the twenty-five bucks for?" Julieta asked.

They sat next to Reuben and me and picked up a kitten each. Hayden held Meggie, and Julieta petted Harry, while Fifi and Johnnycakes hugged each other on top of Reuben. I grabbed Max, and she knew how to curl in the crook of my arm. She fit perfectly with me. Gigi took a look at the empty nest and, after drinking some water, darted in the direction of Mami's room. A swell of emotion roiled over me when I noticed that, like Max, Gigi too was gaining some weight. Her tortoiseshell fur was majestic and shiny. In just a couple weeks, she looked so much better than when I'd first seen her rummaging through the garbage!

"Sometimes people act more responsibly about an animal when they have to pay," I said. "But don't worry, we'll donate the money to the Andromeda Cat Rescue. It's the least we can do for them."

Hayden nodded approvingly.

"But why are you so extra with all the questions?" asked Julieta.

"Because after what the kittens went through the first day of their lives, and how Gigi made sure they were safe with us, as her new human, I have the responsibility and honor to find them perfect placements," I said, fanning myself with a stack of papers. This room was the perfect temperature for the kittens and Beli, but I was burning up.

"Her new human?" asked Julieta, chuckling.

"Yes. Her new human. *Owner* sounds insensitive. Mami

gave me official permission to keep her since her owners up and moved to another country."

Briefly, I told them about the ad and the phone call, and my agreement with Mami.

"Mami said yes?" asked Julieta, awe in her voice.

I narrowed my eyes at her. "And you didn't even need to ask for me," I said.

Hayden, who was hypnotized by Meggie, asked, "Can people apply even if they're not on Astro?"

I thought about it. There was no reason to keep it only school-wide. "People can share the link," I said. "The main photos and videos are on Astro, but the application is on cloud docs. Why? Are you interested?"

Julieta shot me a warning look, but I pretended not to notice her.

Reuben had been listening intently, and when his phone alarm went off, he jumped to his feet. "I have to run now. Keep me updated!"

He carefully put the kittens back in the nest and left.

Julieta and Hayden also put back the babies. Before heading out, Julieta smiled at me and said, "I'm glad you can keep Gigi. And I hope you find the perfect homes for the babies. Let me know if I can help."

I shrugged a shoulder. If I asked her for a favor, she'd want to take over. Julieta was nice but she had her own agenda. Hayden had wanted a kitten forever, and although she hadn't said so, I imagined Julieta thought the kitten would make Hayden think of her, even when she was away at college.

But I was Gigi's favorite; I had to be in charge of placing her babies.

"I'll let you know," I said, and headed to the computer to post the application, along with a picture of each kitten and their names. It was too early to know their personalities when all they did was eat and sleep. But by next week, they should start trying to walk and things would get fun very quickly.

I posted the questionnaire on my FAstro, and on a whim, I sent Papi the link to see what he thought about it.

It seemed Papi was online too because he replied right away, saying that the questions were perfect, that a couple of his companions wanted to apply too, if only they weren't so far away.

Which made me think that there had to be a way to keep everyone happy after the kittens were adopted out. There had to be a way for the interest in helping kittens to continue even after my royal litter was gone.

For now, though, I had to focus on how to select finalists. Reuben and I hadn't talked about a deadline for applications, but I decided to keep it open until the end of January, when I could go through the entries and pick the best candidates.

I felt like I had all the power in the world.

I opened my binder to do my homework, and like a lightning flash, I remembered I'd told Mrs. Thomas that I'd go to school early for language arts, leaving Meera and Bodhi without a ride. How would I tell my mom? What mess had I gotten myself into?

Chapter 10
Support Group

The next morning, I woke up early to feed Max. The kittens slept with satisfied milk-drunken expressions on their faces, except for Max, who turned her face in my direction when she felt me enter the cattery, as Hayden called the laundry room. Max had used the bottle a few times, instead of the syringe, and she had learned to nurse from her mom like a champ. It was so funny to see her fighting for a spot to nurse, pushing the other bigger kittens out of the way.

In a few days, she wouldn't need the bottle anymore. Once her teeth came in at three weeks, she'd be ready to try soft foods. She watched me with such love in her eyes and purred in my hand, and I wished these moments with her wouldn't end.

When the milk was gone, I yawned sleepily as I put Max back in the nest. The cat family lay dreaming under the glow of their nightlight; I'd given them my old rainbow-shaped one. Max crawled in between Meggie and Fifi with so much more coordination than she'd had even yesterday. She'd be walking soon, but for now, they made a kitten hug train as they snuggled with each other. Sister hugs were the best. When I was little, I used to love snuggling with Julieta at night. Until I got too big or we grew too different. I wasn't sure.

I couldn't believe how much the kittens changed each and every day. Johnnycakes nursed round the clock, but the chubbiest was Harry. He had the prettiest heart-shaped white marking right on top of his nose. He looked like a Care Bear wearing a furry tuxedo.

How could I let them go when the time came? I wished there was a way I could keep every one of them. After all, I had been the one working nonstop to keep them safe, to help them thrive. I imagined them living with another family, and an ugly, uncomfortable feeling coiled in my stomach.

The feeling got worse when I remembered I had to tell my mom Mrs. Thomas was waiting for me at school. What would she say? Would she be on my side or Meera's?

Before I was emotionally ready, I found myself knocking at Mami's door half an hour before her alarm went off. During the holidays, she had to be at the store much earlier, but now she'd lose that extra sleep to drive me.

"Come in," she said in a sleepy voice. "What's wrong, Nati?"

I tiptoed to her side of the bed, trying to ignore the ache in my chest seeing Papi's side empty. If he were here, I wouldn't even be in this mess. He'd help me with homework; he'd drive me earlier while Mami drove the Rogers kids.

"Ma," I said, "I forgot to tell you I have to be at school early for a few days. The teacher said. We have to leave now."

Mami was alert in a millisecond. "Baby, you should've told me last night so I could tell Meera and Bodhi to be ready too."

"I don't want to ride with them; I mean, why can't they find another ride, Mami? Mrs. Thomas wants me to arrive early and I couldn't say no."

In Mami's book, a teacher's or a doctor's words were commandments. And giving your word was sacred.

Mami got up from the bed, shaking her head. "Well, I can't leave those children stranded. It's not like they—or you—can walk to school in this weather. It's still dark in the mornings. A neighborhood's a support group. We must help each other. Why are you being so petty?"

Petty? My face flamed. I wished I'd resolved this yesterday. After Mami agreed to let me keep Gigi, I hadn't wanted to ruin the good mood. But I should have known nothing good lasts forever.

Julieta came into the room, ready to leave for school. She looked at me and gave me a brief head shake—clearly, she had heard it all. In my place, she would've done everything so differently. I deserved Julieta's disappointment for making Mami start the day worried, but I hadn't known what else to do.

"Hayden and I can drive her, Mami," my sister said, kissing Mami on the cheek. "Her school is on the way, and it won't be trouble at all."

The expression on Mami's face was brighter than a springtime sunrise. "Really, Juli? Gracias, mi amor," she said. "I'll pick up the kids and head out with Beli to . . ." Mami glanced at me and finished her sentence. ". . . run some errands." It didn't sound like that was what she was going to say. She'd changed her words at the last second.

Her disappointment, I could take. But her lack of trust in me hurt so much.

"What do you mean you're leaving with Beli? Who's going to take care of the babies?" I asked, my voice a lot louder than I expected.

Mami huffed. "The kittens will be fine. Cats live in the wild even in the wintertime, and they survive."

But these were *my* kittens we were talking about, and the mere thought of them home unsupervised for the first time woke up Natalia, Hulk Edition.

"But you'll be in the car with Meera . . ." I said. "What if you mention something about the kittens? Then my whole plan will be ruined."

Mami placed her hands on her waist as she tapped her foot, looking at me with the most infuriating expression. "You and your secrets! They will be fiiiiine." She stretched that *i* as if that would make the word seem more important than it really was. "Now get going before you're late. Mrs. Thomas doesn't get paid for this extra time. Teachers are saints."

I followed Julieta to the front door to wait for Hayden, rolling my eyes at my mom's ridiculous comments. We spoke different languages, and it didn't have anything to do with English and Spanish. And what did she mean by *me and my secrets*?

Despite what I'd said, I trusted my mom *probably* wouldn't let the cat out of the bag. In any case, I had no other choice. It was my fault that Meera would be riding with Beli and Mami without me there to remind them to keep their lips sealed.

A horn honked outside, and I hurried to get in the back

seat of Hayden's red-and-white old-man car. He'd literally inherited it from his grandpa. The car was comfy and warm, and smelled of cinnamon and vanilla, and a little bit of sweat because of his gym bag on the floor of the back seat.

I had to make an effort not to groan when Julieta got in the shotgun seat and kissed Hayden on the lips. Fireworks and sparkles were exploding in his eyes.

"Here," he said, handing her a cup with the logo of her favorite coffee shop. That explained the cinnamon scent, and the cupcake in the cup holder explained the whiff of vanilla.

"Gracias!" she said, and the happiness pulsating from her was kind of adorable, even to me.

"De nada," Hayden said in a surprisingly good accent, his car slowly inching into the street. "And sorry I didn't bring you one, Nati. I didn't see Juli's text that we were driving you until I was already here."

"It's okay," I said, shrugging a shoulder and looking out the window.

"Here," Julieta said, surprising me when she handed me half of her cupcake.

"No, thanks," I said, putting a hand up. "I already ate."

Not that I couldn't have eaten more, but I felt awkward accepting. They were already driving me to school.

"Oh, okay," Juli said with a sad look on her face, which made me want to take the cupcake after all.

Life was so complicated, and it wasn't even seven thirty in the morning yet.

Wanting to break the awkward silence, I asked, "Where are Mami and Beli going?"

Hayden laughed, but at the warning look Julieta shot in his direction, he sobered up real quick.

"What?" I asked, my palms prickling. The hunch that my family was hiding something from me made me nervous. Was it a surprise return of Papi from his deployment? He couldn't show up at school. I would hate crying in front of everyone.

"Mami wants to find a house for Beli," Juli said, and the anxiety building inside me deflated at her words. Was that really what Mami was so secretive about? She and Beli went through the same thing every year, and in the end, Beli never agreed to move out here.

"Beli said yes?" I asked, bursting with the need to know more. But we were already pulling into the school parking lot. "Wouldn't it be great if she stayed here?"

Julieta shook her head. "No. She's only going along so she won't hurt Mami's feelings. Beli would be miserable living here. You know that."

"Yeah, I know," I said, collapsing with a resigned sigh. "But why doesn't Mami know that?"

Hayden and Julieta shrugged in unison as the car stopped at the curb. I clambered out and got all the way to the door before I turned to see them go. I wished I could tag along with Hayden and my sister, that it wouldn't be weird if I hung around with them for the next few months until they started college. Anything but being here so early.

But once inside the classroom, things weren't as bad as I'd feared. There was a track of nature sounds playing and a plate of poppy-seed mini muffins on a little table. I took one and got to work.

It seemed like magic, but when Mrs. Thomas explained the parts of a sentence to me one-on-one, I understood right away. Maybe it was the fact that apart from me, there were only three other kids: Lincoln, Thor, and the prettiest sixth grader in the school besides Meera, Solange Olivier.

I'd never been friends with Solange before, mainly because Meera didn't like her much. Unlike everyone else in the school, Solange hadn't ever bought a tub of slime from Slime Supreme. Instead, she made her own, but she'd never sold it or her secret sparkly formula. I'd always loved the way Solange painted her nails according to the seasons, and how the colors popped against her dark skin, darker than my sister's. Now they were light blue with sparkles that looked like snow. She had a beautiful French accent that made her instantly cool and mysterious. She'd moved here from the island of Saint Martin, which was really close to Puerto Rico.

She caught me staring at her nails, and I smiled

sheepishly, afraid she'd think I was weird. But she smiled too and went back to her work. It must have been hard to attend school in a foreign language. I mean, I'd spoken English all my life, and school was still hard for me. For a while Mami had worried I was confused because she and Papi spoke Spanish, but Julieta never had any issues being bilingual.

I'd never thought about how hard this all was for Solange before, and now I wished that instead of laughing when she pronounced a word the wrong way, I'd offered to help. I would've hated anyone who made fun of my parents or Beli. Why hadn't I said anything to defend her when Meera and her friends laughed at her?

The support group felt like a safe place. No one made fun of each other, and Mrs. Thomas seemed calmer than when she had to wrangle thirty loud students.

Unfortunately, the peace didn't last long. The first bell rang, and the bubble of safe space popped as the rest of the class stampeded in. While everyone settled, I caught the tail ends of conversations.

"I'm going to apply for a kitten," Andrew said, and I was so surprised to hear the words, I held my breath to hear better.

But what he said next felt like a punch in the stomach. "My older brother used to shoot at cats up in the canyon. It's a lot of fun." He laughed, but I flinched.

Shooting cats up in the canyon?

Brigham, his friend, laughed and Andrew added, "With a pellet gun, mind you. It's still fun."

"Bro, the kittens in the video are too small, though," Brigham said. "Besides, what if you don't get one? That application looked so complicated!"

I didn't know much about Andrew, but Brigham had been kind of a bully when we were in kindergarten. Whenever I complained about him, the teacher said he was like a puppy that didn't know his own strength. One day, he pushed me off the swing. I turned around and jabbed him with a one-two-three to the stomach. He never bothered me again, but that's how I ended up at the principal's office for the first time.

"Kittens are cute, and the ones in the video are adorable. But they grow up and turn into pests, you know what I mean?" Andrew continued.

I looked at Andrew and Brigham in disbelief. A part of me wanted to hiss and spit at the boys like a mamacat. Brigham caught my eye, and his pale face reddened until he was the first one who looked away. He wasn't that tough after all.

Andrew noticed the silent war between Brigham and me. "What are you looking at, weirdo?" he asked me.

The second bell rang before I could reply. Mrs. Thomas clapped her hands to call the class to attention, and Andrew, confusing my silence for weakness, smirked and whispered, "Loser."

A couple of rows away, Lilah watched the whole thing with a curious expression on her face.

I looked down at my paper, but I couldn't focus on math when I was so worried about the kittens. I couldn't wait to go through the applications and delete Andrew's as soon as I saw it.

Maybe I should've let the shelter place the kittens, have an adult in charge. This was too hard. I had no idea some people "adopted" pets only to hurt them. If Andrew could be so cruel in public, what was he like in private? What if he got hold of one of my kittens? Or of any kitten for that matter?

I was upset and worried all day long. At resource, after Mr. Warthon explained to me how fractions worked for like the twentieth time, and when he could tell I hadn't understood anything, he patted my hand and said, "Color these pie charts. We'll try again tomorrow, okay?"

The effort of sitting through resource gave me a slight headache. Mr. Warthon was a good teacher, and maybe I'd been too distracted to give him my full attention. I needed to talk to Reuben, but he and Meera had been absorbed exchanging comments on a Barcelona soccer game, as if the goals Messi scored thousands of miles away mattered at all when I had five kittens to protect.

Finally, when it was Meera's turn to work with Mr. Warthon, I made signs to let Reuben know I needed to talk with him. He looked around, as if he were trying to find a way to walk in my direction without being told off. He dropped the pencil off his desk, point first, and it clattered dramatically.

"Oops. I need to sharpen my pencil," he said aloud, in the most obvious voice ever. Anyone could guess that he was trying to hide something.

He stood next to the sharpener—which was conveniently next to my desk—and leaned in my direction. "Today, after school?" he whispered in such a loud voice that it carried all the way to Meera, who looked up in interest.

"Don't be so obvious," I whispered, and in a louder voice, I added, "I'm busy with my grandmother after school. Sorry."

Reuben seemed confused, but I scribbled on my math paper: *Yes, today after school.*

He nodded and went back to his seat and his assignment.

But at the end of the class, I heard Meera ask Reuben, "Why do you spend every afternoon at her house? You haven't come to *my* house in like forever."

"Nothing important," Reuben said, obvious hesitation in his voice, his eyes flickering in my direction.

Meera's eyes got all misty. "Okay," she said, and walked away.

Reuben bit his lip. I didn't know what to tell him, and before I could come up with something, he grabbed his backpack and ran after Meera.

My heart fell all the way to my feet.

For the first time in my life, I understood the concept of fractions. No matter whose side Reuben chose, our trio was broken. A whole broken into three parts. We'd never be one again. And I didn't know how to fix this without asking Reuben to choose either Meera or me. I didn't want to lose the only friend I had.

Chapter 11
Fang, Meet Claw

Like the day before, I walked back home trailing Meera and her friends. I wondered if Bodhi had karate and that's why he wasn't walking home with her. No one else from the class lived on our street, so for the last couple blocks, after she waved Lilah and the other girls goodbye, it was just the two of us on the sidewalk.

I hurried past the corner where the two brindled bull-dogs lived, and when I saw Meera staring back at them over her shoulder, making sure they weren't following her, I felt better. I wasn't the only one scared of them.

I kept hoping she'd slow down so we could, I don't know, talk about what had happened with Slime Supreme. Iron things out, as Beli would say. The whole mess had happened so long ago, though, and Meera had had plenty of opportunities to apologize.

It had been Meera's fault. She should be the one to take the first step. She'd betrayed me—stolen the secret formula that was just mine and Papi's. Why had she chosen to make the other kids happy and ignore how I felt?

In the end, Meera walked into her house, and I went into mine. Would this continue until we moved away for college? The thought depressed me even more.

"Gigi!" I called, and my beautiful, meowgical queen trotted over to say hi. In a heartbeat, she seemed to know how I was feeling. She quickly rubbed my leg with her head. As I pet her, some of the tension in my shoulders evaporated. I followed her back to the cattery, and at the sight of the kittens snuggling close to their mamacat, I wished my life were as simple as theirs. They were trying to wrestle each other, toppling, and rolling, their soft bellies pinkish and round.

Since no one else was home, I lay down on the floor and let the kittens crawl over me. They purred over my chest, and I imagined they were replacing the stress of school with love vibes. My eyes became heavy with sleep. I yawned loudly and the kittens got startled, their tiny claws poking through my T-shirt.

"Ouch!" I complained, and one by one, I put them back in the nest. Now that I was finally alone, I could go through the applications in peace before Reuben arrived soon.

When I woke up the old desktop, I was surprised to see the email notifications in the double digits.

"Yes!" At the sound of Gigi's feet padding toward me, I added, "Look at all the people who want a kitten, Queen G!"

Gigi climbed onto her favorite perch on the shelf next to Papi's picture and looked down at me with an expression that said, *Let's do this!*

The first email I opened wasn't kitten-related, though. It was from Papi, and I read it quickly to make sure he was okay, and then went back to the beginning, putting more attention to reading between the lines.

Nati, the kittens are growing so much! But my favorite one is the mom, Gigi. She's so cute and I bet you once the kittens go to their homes, she'll be super playful and fun. Keep the videos and pictures coming. They make me happy. Who would've thought that I'd become a person who watches kitten videos in between army assignments? Take care of Mami and be good!

    Con amor,

      Papi

Papi didn't always say much, but his presence was so huge, now I felt his absence like a toothache. I *knew* he would be on Team Gigi.

Maybe he missed us—me—as much as I missed him. At least the kitten videos made him happy.

Just when I was getting settled to go through the entries, Gigi jumped from the shelf and ran to the door. A second later, someone knocked. Before I could open it, Reuben's voice came from the other side.

"Knock, knock."

Did he really prepare all these silly jokes or think of them on the spot?

"Who's there?" I asked, really trying not to laugh.

"Interrupting Cat."

Even Gigi looked at me with confusion in her eyes.

"Interrup—"

"Meow, meow, meow!"

I opened the door as he laughed, but I made a show of keeping my face like a mask.

"Interrupting cat, get it?" he said, walking in. The sun had come out, and the melting snow was dripping from the gutters.

"Ah, I get it," I said, my voice laced with sarcasm.

He looked at me and shook his head. "No, you don't, but it's okay." As I expected, he headed into the laundry and came back holding Johnnycakes, who stayed asleep in the crook of Reuben's arm.

"You're going to spoil him, you know?" I asked, sitting down in front of the computer. "You need to socialize with all of them, not only Johnny. Isn't that what you told me the other day?"

Reuben rolled his eyes and went back to the laundry room. Seconds later, he was back with all the kittens. The babies meowed, but they settled quickly on Reuben's lap. Johnny had the place of honor in his arms. Gigi sent him a warning look from the shelf.

"I'll be careful, your meowjesty, Queen Gigi," he said, softly. "Don't take them back, please."

He sat very still, petting Johnny, who hadn't even noticed all his siblings had joined him.

"There are thirty-seven applications," I said, doing a little shimmy in the chair.

Reuben gave me a thumbs-up through a big yawn. Not even five minutes, and the kittens were working their calming magic on him. "Read them," he said, motioning me with a hand to continue.

I scanned the applications as fast as I could, and when I saw Andrew's entry, I gasped.

"What is it?" Reuben asked, his eyes snapping open.

In a few words, I told him about the conversation I'd heard between Andrew and Brigham.

By the end, Reuben's cheeks were bright red, his fist clenched tightly. "Those guys are the worst. Even if they don't get a kitten, we need to tell someone that they think hurting animals is fun."

"Why would he even apply for a kitten?" I wondered angrily. My finger hovered over the delete button. "I'm not even going to read his answers."

"Ouch!" Reuben exclaimed, startling me so bad I pressed down on the delete button.

"What happened?"

Reuben winced as Johnnycakes kneaded his chest, his claws most likely going through the fabric of the Jazz jersey Reuben wore. "Sorry, I didn't mean to scare you, but his nails are sharp!"

"I know," I said, leaning forward to look at the entries. Andrew's was still there. Which one had I deleted? Oops.

Reuben whispered something in Johnnycake's ears that sounded like, "Take it easy, bro."

I tried not to laugh and kept reading a few entries that looked promising, like Jojo's, whose application said she'd never had a pet but that her mom loved cats.

"And listen!" I said, trying not to squeal. "She said she loves Care Bears and Harry looks just like one. I was just thinking that this morning!"

"File her in the maybes, then," Reuben said just as I clicked on the print button. My only answer was the *cha-cha-piiiing* of the printer.

"Smart," Reuben said. "You can go over them carefully if they're printed out."

"Oh! Here's Meera!" I exclaimed when I saw the name on the next application.

Once again, Reuben's cheeks flamed, but this time, it wasn't with indignation like when he'd heard about Andrew.

"She's applying for Bodhi," I said, trying to compose myself as I scanned the rest of the answers.

An uncomfortable silence fell around us. Gigi meowed and twitched her nose.

"Of course she is," Reuben said, the expert on all things Meera. "What else did she write?"

I narrowed my eyes, pretending I had a hard time reading the answers. Maybe I shouldn't have told Reuben about Meera applying for a kitten. Maybe I should've deleted her entry, but the image of Bodhi meowing when he told me how he missed Cap made me feel bad I'd even considered taking him out of the race for a kitten.

I bit my lip and skimmed quickly. "She says her brother has wanted a kitten all his life . . . that they want a cuddly kitten."

"For Bodhi it has to be the cuddliest," Reuben said. He blushed. "You'd better consider them, Natalia."

I didn't know what to say. Part of me had hoped that he'd say I didn't need to consider Meera if I didn't want to, or I don't know, that *I* was his favorite friend. Instead, the silence made me think that he didn't feel safe telling me what he really thought. There was a barrier between Reuben and me. I wished he'd tell one of his silly jokes, but his face looked like his thoughts were a whirlwind.

I wasn't ready to give in yet, but I went along in case my friendship with Reuben depended on what I decided to do with Meera's application.

"Johnnycakes?" I asked, uncertain.

Reuben shook his head, alarmed. "No, Bodhi would go better with Max. She's tiny and gentle and needs the extra attention. You know Bodhi. He'll be pretending she's a magical kitten for the rest of eternity."

The big sigh that escaped me didn't take out all the tension cramping up my shoulders, but I hoped Reuben would understand how hard this situation was for me. "I mean, he calls himself el Niño Gato, so he'd be a perfect candidate. But he's Meera's brother . . ."

Reuben looked up at me and I didn't like the expression on his face. It was too late to take my words back, though. He wouldn't side with Meera now, would he?

"So, let me get this straight," he said, and I braced myself for his next words. "You're going to hurt Bodhi's feelings and dash his hopes of getting a kitten just because you're not talking to Meera?"

"It sounds really bad when you say it that way, Reuben. What I mean is, her actions from last year have to have consequences. She hurt my feelings first, in case you forgot."

"She tried to explain," Reuben said, and when he slapped his hand on the ground, Johnnycakes flinched.

"Aha! Why don't you just say it already? You're on her side too, like the rest of the school."

The kittens were all awake, alert at the words flying back and forth. Reuben must have noticed the tension was like water boiling in Beli's teakettle because he took a long, shuddering breath and said, "Listen, it's already hard enough not to tell Meera I know all about the kittens and Kitten Cupid. She's already upset because I asked you about meeting after school."

"But I said I couldn't after school, which is why you had to come kind of late."

"But here we are," Reuben said, carefully holding all the kittens and standing up.

He didn't add, *And I lied to her,* but I heard it all the same.

"I don't like hiding things from Meera," Reuben said. "She's my friend too. How would *you* feel in her place?"

The vibe in the room was electric. It was clear Reuben wanted to be friends with both of us. But then why was he looking at me like *I* was the bad guy in the movie? I loved Bodhi, but I would never forgive Meera for not putting our friendship first when the other girls pressured us to reveal Caribbean Blue's recipe. How was that so hard for Reuben to understand?

Without another word, Reuben stood up and took the kittens to the laundry. I let him seethe in peace, mainly because I needed a moment to collect myself too. Meanwhile, I kept going through the entries. Solange's name wasn't there, not even applying for someone else, and I was low-key disappointed. Okay, I was high-key disappointed. The fact that she hadn't applied didn't automatically mean she didn't like me—no one but Reuben knew I was the Kitten Cupid. But she seemed like the kind of person who liked cats, just like Bodhi.

Bodhi. How could I ever leave him out no matter how I felt about his sister? I didn't know what to do. Just in case, I printed Meera's entry so I could look it over carefully when I was calmer and Reuben wasn't around to make me feel like the worst person in the world.

The machine came to life, but then a terrible beeping sound broke the silence.

"No!" I said, jumping from my chair and running to the printer to check what was wrong. "Don't give up on me now, printer!"

The screen flashed with a *low yellow ink* warning.

"I don't want to print in yellow! It's black. All black words!" I said, punching buttons to override the message. But the words kept flashing.

"Reuben," I called over my shoulder, feeling frustrated about more than just the printer.

Reuben came out of the laundry room with a sad expression on his face that I didn't know how to read.

"Can you help?" I pointed at the computer. "If it makes you feel any better, I'm trying to print out—"

His phone buzzed. He answered, and even feet away, I could hear his mom's voice.

"Bueno, Mamá," he said. "Heading back now."

There was a rapid-fire reply on the other side, and through clenched teeth, he said, "Bueno. Ahora vuelvo, I said." Pause. "Mami," he added in a softer voice.

By the annoyed expression on his face, I could tell his mom must have been on a Spanish-only kick. Mami hadn't been on me about speaking only Spanish for a few weeks, but that didn't mean it wasn't coming for me too.

I gave Reuben a smile of sympathy, but he seemed too out of sorts to smile back. "I gotta go," he said. "The kittens will need shallow litter boxes soon, FYI. I think Harry just went on the blanket. You'll have to change it before it smells."

I tsked. Things were getting to be interesting while Gigi hopefully potty-trained the kittens. "Okay, I'll do that, and then I'll finish the applications. People have until the thirty-first anyway. So . . . see you here tomorrow?"

Reuben was already heading out the door. "I can't. If I come over three days in a row, Meera will get suspicious. She'll start asking questions, and I don't want to lie to her."

All I heard was that there was a huge chance he'd tell Meera about everything.

In typical Natalia fashion, I reacted by bringing out fang and claw. "If you tell her it's me behind the kittens, she will tell the whole school just like she posted my secret recipe, and then everyone will know—"

Reuben opened the door but turned around and said, "Do you really not trust me at all? You can't imagine how hard it's been standing in the middle of you two."

A worm of unease burrowed into my stomach, and I hated the image that popped in my mind. Reuben being pulled from side to side.

"She'll understand."

Reuben just stared back and I squirmed. Wanting to change the subject, I said, "Look, I had this great idea for tomorrow. I think it will be cute to do a kitten Olympics event on live FAstro to show their personalities better. I want people to be able to pick which one they'll get along with best. What do you think?"

Reuben chewed on his bottom lip and said, "Sure, but we probably shouldn't try to do that for another two or three weeks. The kittens need to be confident on their feet and running around."

"Okay, then," I said, shrugging one shoulder. "Three weeks, to make sure. That's after Beli leaves." When he didn't react, I said in a singsongy voice, "No quesitos."

"It's okay," he said, and left without making a single joke.

Just as he was leaving, practically running away from my house, Mami and Beli were coming back. Even from the front door, I could see their unhappy faces as Mami headed to the carport. They'd been arguing.

Great. Just what I needed.

Chapter 12
The Coquí Song and the Maga Flower

Mami and Beli brought the chill of a polar vortex with them. Even Gigi felt the bad vibes and, after a quick glance at the situation, darted into the laundry, where she stayed away from the drama. She was a smart girl.

As soon as she came in, Mami saw the printer flashing.

"Natalia!" she called in a loud voice that would definitely count as yelling if *I* used it. "Stop printing things out! We can't keep up with the toner, which isn't exactly cheap, young lady!" She kept muttering unintelligibly while I tiptoed my way to my room to wait out the storm. She must have touched something because the printer sounded like it was coming back to life.

If the machine started printing again, the first thing it would spit out would be the entries, with Meera's on top.

I had to get the papers before Mami saw them, or she'd start asking and asking until I told her all the secrets about the matches and the Astro. Mami would get involved with the kittens and make things worse. She wouldn't understand about the anonymous account.

Mami went into her room and locked her door. It wasn't a door slam, but the sound of that lock was like that of a wall coming up. If she was sad, I wished she'd tell me. I wished we could talk it out. Instead, everyone was sad on her own.

I waited in my room until I saw Beli go into the kitchen. She was curiously quiet, not listening to her music on her phone and singing along. It was around the time she started making dinner every day, but the kitchen remained silent and cold. What was going on?

I ventured out with the excuse of having to go to the bathroom, when I saw the printer was unsupervised and

Meera's entry was right there on top of the tray. I ran to snatch the papers, and on the way back to my room, I saw Beli sitting in the kitchen, petting Gigi, who sat on her lap. Beli had such a sad expression on her face that I couldn't ignore her. Just in case, I put the papers in my room first.

When I came back, my grandma was still sitting in the same position, looking out the window at the snow gently falling. I didn't hate the winter as much as Beli did, or at all, really. We needed the moisture if we wanted a green spring—and a safe summer. Late last summer right after the start of the school year, we'd had many wildfires along the dry Wasatch mountains. A yellow toxic bubble of smoke covered the Utah Valley, where Andromeda was nestled. Principal Snow had declared inside recess for weeks. Not that it mattered to me—I'd been spending a lot of time alone in the library—but still, it was miserable to be cooped inside with so many other sixth graders.

Even if she hadn't said it a million times a day, I knew Beli loathed this weather. The sky was dark gray, and there was no mistaking the sigh that seemed to come from the very bottom of her heart.

"What's wrong, Beli?" I asked, taking her hand in mine.

She smiled sadly, and I dropped her hand to go turn the light on. Now I could see her dark brown eyes were damp. She sighed again. "I just wish I could be in two places at once."

Was this what Reuben was feeling earlier today?

"You're ready to go home?" I sat next to her and placed my head on her shoulder.

Beli caressed my hair with her hand. "Ay, mi amor. I feel like the island's calling me. I'm like el coquí."

El coquí is a tiny tree frog that's also Puerto Rico's national animal. The legend Papi used to tell me every night said that it couldn't live outside the island. That when it was too far from its shores, it stopped singing until it died.

I hugged Beli tightly. "Don't say that."

Beli must have heard the fear in my words because she added, "I'm like a flor de maga, then."

"The what?"

"The Puerto Rican amapola, mi niña. Remember the big red flower with the long yellow center? If I spend too long in the cold, something in my heart starts shriveling, like the flower that misses the sunshine and the warmth."

"You're going home soon," I said. "Just a few more days."

Beli sighed, and I sat up to look at her eyes. "Yes, mi amor, and how I wish I could stay with Gina and you girls."

"Tío Mako must miss you too, though," I said, lowering my eyes so she didn't see the hurt in mine. Unlike Mami, I tried never to tell Beli how unfair it felt that his family had more time with her than we did. Still, the unsaid words made a knot grow painfully in my throat.

Beli lifted my chin with a finger so I couldn't hide from her. "Yes, when I'm here, Mako and the girls miss me, and I miss them. When I'm there, I miss you and you miss me, but it was important to be here with you for the holidays with your papi gone. It's never easy when the family is scattered from each other like little seeds. I could never love either one of my children more than I love the other."

My smile was tinged with sadness. "Mami always says

the same thing about me and Juli, but it doesn't look that way to me. Everyone has a favorite."

"Really?" Beli asked. "Do you think Gigi spends more time with Max than with Johnnycakes because she prefers one over the other?"

I shook my head. The truth was that, no, I didn't believe Gigi had a favorite kitten. She spent more time with Max because the tiny kitten needed more attention than her siblings. Meggie and Fifi, for example, were low-maintenance because they were doing well without extra help. The other day, though, Julieta had been sweeping too close to where Meggie was playing, and Gigi had jumped and attacked the broom with a ferocious yowl.

Beli said, "Do you love your papi or your mami more? Me or your mami?"

I bit my lip, not knowing how to reply. It was easy being angry at Mami because she was the only one around, but honestly, I knew that no matter what problem I got into, my mom loved me. Just like she knew Beli loved her, even if she didn't move into the cold weather with us.

"Mami's favorite is Juli. You can't deny it," I said, and the words hurt when they left my lips.

Beli shook her head. "Don't you remember how those two used to argue when Julieta was your age?"

I scoffed. Juli and Mami in a fight? They had their little disagreements, but nothing like the arguments with me. Beli never lied, but it was hard to believe her this time.

She continued, "Every day Julieta complained that you were the favorite because Gina was always having to go to doctor's appointments with you, and"—Beli's face lit up as she remembered—"you slept in your parents' bed until you were six years old!"

I felt heat rising from the tip of my toes to the ends of my hair. I laughed. "I remember! But it was only on stormy nights!"

Beli cupped my face with a hand. "You needed more attention. Like Max. It never was about either one being the favorite."

Leave it to Beli to make everything better. "You're always my favorite grandma," I said, hugging her again.

"I'm your only grandma!" She laughed and hugged me back. "You remind me so much of your mom, you have no idea."

"You always say that, pero, Beli, I don't see it," I said, sitting up.

"You're both opinionated and passionate. And," she said, pecking my nose with a kiss, "you have a knack for protecting the innocent. Once when she was your age, your mother brought home a tiny chick, and she begged me to keep it. I couldn't say no. The thing is, the chick grew and became a beautiful rooster."

"A pet rooster?" I exclaimed as so many things fell into place. That's why Mami had been so upset when the raccoon ate Mrs. Lind's chickens!

"That bird loved her and followed her all over the house. I loved seeing it perched on her shoulder, and I loved it even more when it chased the dog, Bandit, out of the compost pile in the yard."

I laughed, Beli's words making a movie in my mind of my mom, her rooster, and her dog.

"What happened to it?" I asked.

Beli shrugged. "It lived a long, beautiful life . . . until the neighbor's cat got to it." I clapped my hand to my mouth to stifle a cry. Beli explained, "Since then, your mom hasn't been a fan of cats. She hated them when Hayden's cats scratched Julieta's arm."

"Then why did she let me keep Gigi and the babies if she hates cats?"

In that moment, though, Mami walked into the kitchen, Gigi in her arms, and said, "Because I love you, and this precious animal needed help. If the little girl inside me found out I'd kicked out an animal in need, even a cat, she'd have never forgiven me." Gigi looked up at Mami and mewed. "Besides, look at this queen's face."

"Gracias, Mami," I said. "Beli, next time come see us in the summertime."

Beli laughed. "I'll do that." Then she bit her lip and checked the clock. "Mira la hora! And I haven't even started the mofongo I was going to make. Tomorrow the plantains might be too ripe."

"We'll make amarillos, then," I said. Sweet plantains in syrup was the food of the gods.

"Yes, amarillos for dinner!" Mami exclaimed, and for a second, it looked like the little girl she'd been was peeking out through her brown eyes. "For now, though, what about takeout? Taco Tuesday?"

Beli beamed at Mami. "Tacos are a good idea every day," she said, and they hugged in silence for a long time, Gigi squished between them.

Later, after my tummy was happy, I left Mami and Beli softly talking in the kitchen. Snatches of their conversation drifted to me, like when Beli explained her life was in Puerto Rico, her job in the school where she cooked. But that she left knowing we'd be okay until Papi came back.

Juli and Hayden showed up soon after with chocolate chip cookies Hayden's mom had sent, and after grabbing a couple, I went to my room to go over more applications.

I took Max and Fifi, who never got as much attention, and a pink ball of yarn from Beli's craft bag. The two sisters were playing when Hayden peeked into my room and said,

"There she is. I was looking for Fifi. Can I trade you?" He held Meggie in his other hand.

"Sure," I said, eager to go back to my task.

As soon as she was on the floor, Meggie pounced on Max. The pair was too cute, and I grabbed Julieta's camera from under my bed and snapped a picture.

"Oooh," Hayden said, pointing at the camera. "There it is. Juli was looking for the camera the other day."

My whole body felt like it was in flames. "Oops, don't tell her, please. I'll put it back. I promise," I said. "I just need to upload the photos to the computer first."

Hayden wagged a finger at me and said, "Don't forget."

I narrowed my eyes. "Listen, Hayden," I whispered. "Remember I'm the one making decisions on who's going to get a kitten and which one. I see you're too attached to Fifi, so watch your mouth."

Hayden clutched Fifi against his chest. "Rude," he said. "And besides, you want them to end up with the best candidate ever, right? You can't let your prejudices or your ego come before the kittens' well-being. That is, if you care about them." He turned on his heels and went back to the kitchen. With Fifi!

He was such a clown, and he liked using long words. He was worse than Reuben even, but he had a point. Or two. I had to return Julieta's camera somehow. I gave her a hard time, and if the roles were reversed, I'd be annoyed at my little sister taking everything from me. The truth was, she always had my back. She'd driven me to the vet that first night; she'd bought cat food and litter without me having to ask her; she asked Hayden to drive me to school so I didn't have to ride with Meera.

And choosing the best candidates? He was right about that too. Bodhi and his whole family were one of the best options for a kitten. So what if he was Meera's brother? Would I let the past get between one of the kittens and fur-ever happiness?

Reluctantly, I finally took a close, serious look at Meera's application.

1. Personal information: *Meera Rogers*

2. All members of your household: *My dad, my mom, my little brother, and me. Sometimes my grandparents, and lots of friends, come to visit, but all kids are well behaved around animals.*

That was true. Meera's house was always full, but I remembered a birthday party where Cap had been the center of everyone's gentle attention.

3. Do you have any animals?: *A dog, Captain America, who passed away in December. He had cancer and was in a lot of pain. So we had to put him down. It was our duty as his humans to make sure he wasn't hurting. He didn't deserve all that pain. He was the best dog and friend ever. He was a rescue and lived with our family since I was in kindergarten.*

Poor Meera. Cap had looked so sick at the vet. I didn't understand how a person could make the hard decision to let a pet go, but maybe what she said was true, that as their humans, it was our responsibility to let them go to animal heaven in peace. An act of kindness for all the love so freely given. If that were ever the case with Gigi, would I be brave enough to let her go? My mind said yes, but my heart cried no. If that moment came, though, I hoped to do the right thing.

Something that felt like respect bloomed in my chest for Meera and her family.

I kept reading, but my attention zeroed in on answer number six:

> *I'm interested in adopting a kitten because my little brother has wanted one his whole life. He's been so sad since Cap died and asks for a kitten every day! My parents have said yes but haven't taken us to the shelter yet. It would make him so happy, and I have been feeling lonely too. I loved Cap, and it would be hard to have another dog. So I think a kitten would be a great option. My brother and I love every photo of the kittens, and we could give one of them a lot of love.*

I jumped to answer number eight:

> *I'd love Max, especially because she was so much smaller and frailer than the other kittens, but look at her now! Bodhi is so gentle, and I think he would like a really cuddly kitten.*

I put the papers down, trying not to groan. She wanted Max? *My* Max? Maybe asking people to write down their choices had been a mistake. Maybe trying to find homes for the kittens had been a mistake.

I flipped through the other applications, wondering what to do. I came to Lilah's application—she'd sided with Meera immediately last year. I skipped right to number six.

> *I'd love a kitten because I'm home alone a lot of the time now. My older siblings have moved out, and now I feel like an only daughter. My first niece was born two weeks ago, and my parents spend a lot of time going back and forth to help my brother and his wife, my sister-in-law. My nephews (from my other*

brothers) are too young to be my friends, and my sib-
lings are too old for us to have anything in common.
I would have so much time and attention for one of
the kittens.

My heart panged. Not every person who felt lonely was the best candidate for a kitten . . . right?

Sighing, I put the papers down. Something furry brushed my skin and tickled me. At my feet, Max and Meggie attacked each other and rolled in a hug until the leg of the bed stopped them. Max glared up at the hanging bedspread and attacked it instead. She looked like a kitty Tarzan, and soon Meggie joined her in their game of swinging from the bedspread. For being so tiny, Max sure was the mastermind.

In that moment, Julieta came into my room, and when she saw the kittens hanging from the bed, she covered her mouth and said, "Oh my gosh, Nati! If Mami sees them . . ."

She didn't need to end that sentence. The silky fabric had four sets of tiny-but-obvious rips that I wouldn't be able to hide with anything.

"Oops," I said. "Don't tell, Juli, please. Five more weeks, and I'll have to let them go."

"Five? More like six." Juli's eyes softened. She picked up the kitty sisters and kissed them on top of their heads. When she looked at me, she grimaced. "And you might want to check the nest. Harry keeps going on the blanket."

She left with kittens in hand, and I turned the comforter around so the tears on the fabric wouldn't be the first thing Mami saw when she entered my room.

Five-ish weeks to go. Would the house and my family survive the kittens in one piece?

Chapter 13
Playing Angry Tag

Between support group before class, school, and taking care of the kittens, the next few days flew by; they tumbled into each other, and before I knew it, weeks had passed. In that time, Meera's parents told my mom she didn't need to drive the kids anymore. I felt almost guilty for avoiding the car rides together. Every time I saw Bodhi at school, he stopped to tell me something about the Kitten Cupid videos. He was obsessed.

My heart was a battle zone.

During that time, I turned in my paper to Mrs. Thomas. I'd written about the shelter's need for volunteers and had included the lost pet ad from Gigi's previous family.

Without going into too much detail, I wrote about kittens that didn't make it without the help of volunteers and foster families. When Mrs. Thomas returned the paper, I saw a *100%* in pink marker, and the smile on her face made me blush with satisfaction.

She winked at me but didn't comment aloud to the class. I wondered about that smile and the wink every time I checked on my FAstro to load a new video or photo.

In less exciting news, during that time Reuben stopped by the house only once, and I suspected he did because it was Beli's last night before heading back to Puerto Rico.

I had wanted to set up the Kitten Olympics, with obstacle courses I'd designed when I was supposed to be practicing math facts. I was sure it would help bring out their personalities, even if I already felt I knew each of them so well. But he wasn't any help at all. While I connected boxes and plastic tubes with duct tape, he just played with the kittens the whole time.

When he kept brushing away my comments about lining up the kittens for a race or swinging the string for the catch-the-feather game, I switched tactics. I suggested we go over the rest of the applications. I still wasn't sure who the finalists were.

"Put me down for Johnny. You know I'm his favorite," Reuben said in a quirky voice.

That boy couldn't do anything serious.

When he started throwing jokes around, it meant nothing would get done. Something was brewing in Reuben's mind, but I didn't know what.

The only moment he became interested in what I was doing was when I told him Brigham's had been one of the two applications that arrived right under the wire the night before. His answers had been surprisingly sweet. I hadn't read Hayden's yet.

"Really? You're going to believe anything Brigham writes? He's Andrew's minion!" Reuben complained, red-faced as he tried to shake off Harry, Meggie, and Fifi, who were trying to climb his jeans legs. They looked like mountain climbers struggling to reach Mount Everest's summit. Johnnycakes watched them smugly from his throne on Reuben's arms.

"They look like they want to eat you," I said, fascinated at how determined the kittens were. I'd never seen them act this way other than when they smelled Beli's cooking. "What did you touch before coming here?"

Reuben smiled sheepishly and said, "I was helping my mom with the arepas filling for tonight."

"Now they think you're a giant arepa." I laughed.

"I promise I washed my hands," he said, finally plucking off one kitten at a time. Meggie had found the feather toy and was shredding it, and each of her siblings tumbled over to join her. I would be cleaning up feather bits for days. At six weeks old, they were all menaces; bringing all of them out at once was a questionable choice. Fifi pounced onto Gigi's stomach and she howled in protest.

"They're kind of a handful even for Gigi," I said, laughing.

"No kitting!" Reuben replied, and for a second, it seemed like everything was back to normal. Almost.

Until he remembered Brigham's application. "Honestly," he said. "It doesn't matter that he wants a kitten for his little brother. Have you ever seen Trevyn? He's just Brigham 2.0, the meaner and crueler version. Ask Bodhi what he thinks of him."

"Maybe a kitten is what he needs to calm down," I said, biting my pencil. Not that I was even remotely considering Brigham, but the fact that Reuben had assumed I was made me angry, so I kept going. "A kitten's not supposed to be a reward for being nice . . . I don't know. Maybe Trevyn needs a kitten to learn about kindness."

Reuben just stared at me. "If you give him any of our kittens, Natalia, I will never talk to you again."

Reuben exaggerated all the time. This time, though, there was a seriousness behind the words that chilled me. Reuben had been my only constant friend all this time, and the days without him had been almost unbearable. But why would he talk to me this way?

"Ours?" I snarled. "They're *my* cats, Reuben Francis, and *I* make the choices. I have the power!" In my defense, the expression sounded funny in my mind. But he didn't take it that way. He didn't even smile. Instead, his chin quivered, and silently, he gathered the kittens and began leading them to the laundry room like a pied piper. Gigi saw her chance and stayed in the kitchen, seeking refuge under Beli's legs as she made dinner. Beli sent me a questioning look, and I shrugged, feeling worse than if she'd told me off.

"Hey," I said when Reuben came back. "It was a joke."

"I'm not laughing. How many times have you told me that if no one laughs, then it's not a joke?" he said, wringing his hands as if he wanted to tell me something else but didn't know how.

I was scared of what he'd say, so I spoke first. "Don't you have to be at your best friend's now? Careful she doesn't think you like me better, you know?" He looked so confused, so I added, "Meera, yes. I'm talking about her. Don't look so surprised. You never come over anymore, and when you do, it looks like you can't wait to tell me you need to go. So go, Reuben!"

The silence that followed was louder than the roar of an airplane engine. Beli looked up, but she didn't say anything.

Reuben walked over to where she was, kissed her on the cheek, and said, "Have a great flight back home, Beli."

And he left without looking back at me or even saying goodbye.

Later, when I was doing dishes, Beli picked up a towel and started drying the pans. She'd been cooking for days, not only for tonight but to last us weeks. The fridge and freezer were packed. If she couldn't be here, at least we'd be well fed. If that wasn't an act of love, I didn't know what was.

Her suitcases sat by the door, and soon she and Mami would be heading to the airport for her to catch the red-eye flight to New York City and then on to San Juan.

I sighed, and Beli pulled me close with an arm.

"Te voy a extrañar, mi chiquita," she said in a husky voice.

I knew it was true that she would miss me. Not as much as I'd miss her, though. Without her, I'd be by myself most of the time. It'd be just the cats and me. Mami and Julieta had their own lives, and Reuben was acting all weird. I didn't understand him anymore.

"Have a great trip, Beli" was all I managed to say. I knew she'd be happy back home, in her little house by the beach with Tío Mako's canary Pichuco singing to her in the mornings. She'd be happy with her cafecito and pan soba'o, and here I'd be with my reheated quesitos and empanadillas. At least I'd have my kittens. But only for a few more days, and then they'd be gone too.

She kissed me on the cheek and said, "I left you a present on your bed. I hope you love it."

"You're sure you're not coming to the airport?" Julieta asked, pausing in the doorway.

I shook my head. For a second, I regretted telling Mami that I'd rather stay home, but even the thought of Beli leaving made my eyes prickle with tears. If I actually saw her leaving, who knew if I'd ever stop crying?

I'd gone to the airport to see Papi off when he left in September, and I wasn't ever going to put myself in that situation again. I couldn't avoid the sadness of someone else's absence, but I could avoid the drawn-out airport goodbye.

"Nati, I can't find my camera. Have you seen it? I wanted to get some nice shots at the airport," Juli said.

Her question startled me so badly I dropped a cup and it shattered in the sink. "Oops," I said, but my bright cheeks must have been the proof she needed to know I was hiding something.

Her eyes looked just like Reuben's when I'd told him to go to Meera's.

"Give it back, Natalia," Julieta said, her hand facing up, her foot tapping on the floor.

"I don't have it," I said.

Beli cleared her throat, and I sighed.

I could just barely deal with Papi being gone so long, Reuben being mad at me, and having to say goodbye to the kittens, but not with Beli looking so disappointed in me. I couldn't let her go thinking Julieta and I were fighting.

I stomped to my room and saw a big box on top of the comforter. I'd open it later, when I wasn't upset. Maybe I didn't deserve this present with how I'd behaved with my sister. I rummaged in my closet for the camera and headed back to the kitchen with it.

Julieta and Beli had been mumbling by the door. Mami was already out in the car.

"Here," I said, handing the camera to my sister.

Julieta took it, and the first thing she did was turn it on, like she wanted to see if I'd broken it.

She looked up at me and said, "I would've happily lent you the camera if you asked, you know? Why did you take it? I can't ever trust you, Natalia."

She didn't even sound angry, so I couldn't react defensively. My sister was right, and not even Beli could side with me in this argument.

Mami honked outside, and without another word, Julieta headed out.

My heart fluttered like a butterfly that fell to the ground with the heavy rain. The wings of my heart were machucadas, bruised with so many bumps.

Beli hugged me one last time and said, "You know, gatos are adorable. But pushing everyone else away, playing angry tag, won't make you happy, Nati. Think about that." She kissed my forehead and smiled. "Remember I'm hashtag Team Natalia all the way."

Before I could promise I'd try again, that I wouldn't let my fears turn me into a sour lemon, Beli went out to the car. She'd left the box of dominoes she loved on the table, like a promise that soon she'd be back.

For a while, I played with the kittens and tried to get them to run the obstacle course. Herding kittens by myself was impossible, though. After playing all day, they fell asleep one by one, wiped out from all their adventures. I tried to scoop up Max to cuddle with her, but Gigi sent me a look that I interpreted as *don't you dare*, so instead, I picked up the applications I'd printed out and went over them again and again.

So many people wanted a kitten, not only from school but from all over the neighborhood. It was so hard to know how to choose. How to choose right. I browsed Astros trying to catch glimpses of people's lives, but in their regular accounts, they only posted the best for the world to see. It was in the

FAstros, with made-up names, that they showed who they really were. Why did we all hide behind screens and fake accounts?

I got a headache and turned off the computer and went back to the printouts. Hayden's application was perfect, going over his story about Bagheera and Catsby, and how much he loved them. After five years without them, he figured it was about time to try again. He thought having a kitten at his parents' house would be calming while he did all his work for college. He, of course, wrote down Fifi as his first pick.

Other applications were easy to throw in the garbage. For example, Saylor said that her main reason for adopting was to transform the kitten into a social media celebrity.

"I don't think so," I said, crushing the paper and tossing it in the garbage.

After a while, only a handful of applications made the final list. I stacked them on the table: Jojo and Hayden were solid yeses. Meera's and Lilah's were off to the side. Every time I decided to take them out of the pile, something inside me stopped me. It was like a whisper telling me to reconsider. Even if both of them had been mean to me, they might be the best for one of the kittens.

Beli's words not to play angry tag rang in my memory along with Hayden's warning not to let my prejudices and ego get in the way of the kittens' fur-ever happy families.

I wished I could call Reuben, that we could discuss this like we normally would. He'd become so irrational when I'd jokingly said Brigham might be a good candidate, I was afraid that if I mentioned I was considering Lilah, very loosely, he wouldn't speak to me again. And if I told him I'd chosen Bodhi and Meera, would he be relieved or just tell me "I told you so"?

Life was so complicated!

If only everything was naps and cuteness like with the kittens. Crushed by loneliness and the need to talk to some-one, I checked back on my FAstro. Even if I wanted to stay away from it, looking at it was like an itch I just had to scratch. Even when I'd just been a lurker, it had helped to see what everyone else was doing. Now that I could be in on the action, even if no one knew who I was, I felt part of everything again.

There were hundreds of views of the latest kitten video. It was one of my favorites to date. Beli caught it by sheer luck on her phone and emailed it to me, and after I made sure I didn't appear on the video at all, I'd uploaded it to my feed.

Mami had asked me to vacuum the kitchen and living room, but as soon as I turned on the vacuum, Gigi arched her back, hissed, and started stalking me. The five kittens, even Max, were watching me vacuum with curiosity and fear. I didn't see Gigi give the order to attack, but at once, the six cats jumped on the vacuum's hose and started trying to take it down.

At first, I'd been in shock at how earnest they seemed in bringing down the beast.

How long had they been planning the attack? I imagined Gigi speaking to them when they were newly born, preparing them for the moment when they'd all jump the red dragon.

I smiled now remembering how I'd laughed with Beli yesterday when she had to stop recording.

These tiny creatures had brought so much happiness into my life. How was I going to say goodbye to them? Especially to Max. I didn't dare ask Mami if I could keep her too, but the truth was, I wanted her for myself. Maybe I could wait up and ask, but they'd be back super late, and Mami wouldn't be in the mood to argue.

Mami and Juli would wait for Beli's airplane to take off at midnight, to make sure she was safely on her way. Besides, I had a long day at school tomorrow, so I went to bed.

On my bed awaited Beli's present, like hope wrapped in printed paper of kittens and crowns. How in the world she'd found this paper, I'd never guess.

Careful not to tear the wrapping paper, I opened the package. My fingers prickled at the touch of wool inside the box. I took out seven sweaters made of the same bright pink yarn I'd seen hanging from Beli's purse like a tail. Five of the sweaters were a tiny bit too big for the kittens now, but they'd fit perfectly when it was time for them to go home in a week. Another one was perfect for Gigi, and then the last one was for me. They all had the same heart design with tiny triangular ears on top. The design on mine was in the front, and the cats' on the back. A paper flew down from my sweater. I unfolded it and recognized Beli's elegant loopy handwriting immediately.

Beli had never written me a letter before.

Nati Natalia,

I made these sweaters for los gatitos and for you while you were at school. I think they'll be the perfect going-to-their-fur-ever-home outfits, and I think you'll look beautiful in one too. I hope you fix this speed bump on the road of friendship with Reuben. Having a friend is a treasure. Having one like Reuben is such an abundance. Why do you keep pushing him away?

I'm glad you have your gatita to keep you company. You and your mami will need each other more than ever. Your mami and Julieta have a special bond. It was just the two of them for a long time until your papi came along. But it doesn't mean your mami doesn't adore you just like I adore her.

I'm not leaving because I love your tío Mako and your primas more than I love you and your mom and sister. I'm leaving because I'm needed at home. Goodbyes are sad, but think about our hug when we see each other next!

Keep me updated on all things gatitos. Send me a picture or two of you and Gigi. She's busy with her babies now, but once she gets the chance to be a pampered kitten for the first time in her life, I know she'll be a great companion and friend.

Con amor,

Abuela Beli

I read the letter twice and put it inside my planner.

Gigi meowed, and I made room in the bed for her. Tomorrow at school, I'd ask Solange why she hadn't applied. Maybe I could convince her to give kittens a try. And maybe I'd be able to confide in Reuben and tell him Bodhi was one of the finalists for the kittens even if I couldn't forgive Meera. Tomorrow would be a new day.

Chapter 14
The Kitten Wars

At school, it was hard to find a moment to talk to Reuben without Meera overhearing. Once or twice, I was sure he'd noticed me making signs at him, but he pretended not to see. After a couple times when he plainly saw me and ignored me, I stopped trying to get his attention.

I just didn't understand why he was mad at me. Was he still offended because he had to keep a secret from Meera? He'd never been that offended with her for not keeping mine.

The days went by, and I had no one to talk to about the hardest decision in my life. Beli was there for me, just a phone call away, but it just wasn't the same.

The one thing that almost made up for having to keep

the secret was having proof of how much Andromeda Elementary's mood had improved since the Kitten Cupid had taken over Astro. One day at lunch, Solange, Lilah, and Jojo were squealing over Max's new video and Harry's photos of him wearing a tiny crown.

"The videos are the highlight of my day," Solange said, twirling her hair around her finger.

"That little Max is a spunky one!" said Lilah, with longing in her voice.

"I wish I could kiss that tiny adorable Care Bear face," said Jojo with a wistful expression on her face. "I love how he washes his face in the videos, have you seen him?"

Lilah replied, "I have no idea how the person raising them decides who they go to, though. Do you think you know who it is?"

My heart pounded as I tried to hear Jojo's answer without looking like I was eavesdropping on them.

"It has to be someone with access to AstroSnap, my sister said. Most likely, an adult is making all the videos and captions," Jojo said.

"The graphics aren't that great, though," Solange said, and Jojo and Lilah agreed.

It was almost impossible not to scream to the four walls of the lunch room that I'd done it all without help, bad graphics and all. But instead of letting the cat out of the bag, I threw the rest of my sad cafeteria lunch away and walked to PE, feeling like I was floating.

Everyone loved the videos, but having to choose the families was the worst. I'd started out so excited to pick the kittens' new owners, but I hadn't expected to feel so much pressure. I wanted the drama and stress to end, but at the same time, I didn't want the moment to arrive when I'd have to say goodbye to the kittens for good.

The night before the big announcement was supposed to go out, I hardly slept, and in the morning, I lost track of time in the shower trying to make up my mind, comparing kittens and people, matching their differences and similarities. I'd been so immersed in my thoughts that I hadn't noticed the bathroom was thick with vapor, and I had to open the bathroom window to let it out so I could see myself in the mirror.

Mami had left earlier than usual, and I didn't even get to talk to her. With Valentine's weekend upon us, I didn't expect she'd be home much. She'd said this year they had record orders for arrangements. Besides, I wanted to show her I could take care of placing the kittens without having to involve her, like I'd promised.

But I was distracted all day, and during resource class, I almost missed the conversation happening between Andrew and Reuben. I was glad my ears caught the urgency of their voices, and I stopped working on my math problems.

"Yes," Reuben said, "I applied for one too. Did you?"

I put my pencil down and stared at Reuben. He'd been making jokes about Johnnycakes, but he hadn't applied. Now, though, why would he lie about it to Andrew?

His cheeks were bright red when he lifted his gaze and realized I was looking at him.

Had he applied for a kitten, then? The answer was plain on his face, but I'd never seen his application. I looked at Andrew next, and he must have felt my eyes on him because he looked over his shoulder, and when he saw me, he smirked.

"I applied the first day. I wonder how we'll know when we're getting one," Andrew said. "Do you think they'll message us on Astro today like they said or was it all a hoax?"

"*If* you're getting one, you'll get a message," Reuben corrected him. "It's not a hoax, but if I were you, I wouldn't hold my breath."

It was the wrong thing to say. Andrew puffed up like the puffer fish in the library's fish tank, making himself bigger than he already was.

"And why do you think I won't get one? It's not like I'm that weirdo Natalia," Andrew said. "Brigham applied too, for his brother, Trevyn. What kind of person wouldn't agree to give a kitten to a first grader?"

"The kind of people who know Trevyn," Meera said without taking her eyes off her paper.

Andrew clenched his fists, and his face was red and splotchy. "What did you just say?"

I almost yelled for Meera to be careful—who knew what Andrew could do when he got upset?—but it wasn't necessary. In that moment, Reuben stepped in between Andrew and Meera, protecting her.

Mr. Warthon heard the commotion and came to our corner of the room. He looked at me and asked, "What's wrong?"

There was no reason for him to ask *me*. I hadn't even said anything, but I guess he was just like everyone else, blaming me because of the past. I glanced from Andrew to Reuben to Meera, and back at Andrew.

What could I tell the teacher? That we were arguing about kittens? If the teachers found out about my FAstro, it wouldn't be hard for the rest of the truth to come out. And if I didn't confess, it was only a matter of time before anyone else discovered my almost eight-week-old secret. The truth was just as hard to contain as the kittens themselves.

Soon, the kittens would be adopted, and then no one would care about Kitten Cupid or my FAstro anymore. A few more hours and I'd be free of the whole thing that, instead of bringing me kindness or happiness, had created so much trouble.

"So?" Mr. Warthon repeated his question. "Everything okay?"

"Everything's okay," I said, and went back to my worksheet.

But Andrew was way smarter than I'd ever given him credit for. After resource, I saw him heading to the office, and soon I'd find out why.

During language arts, we had a sub, and we were supposed to be doing silent reading when I overheard Brigham and Andrew talking about the kittens—but that wasn't all.

"It has to be her," Andrew was saying. "I mean, if you compare the style of her graphics and fonts to her normal Astro, they're practically identical."

Each of his words was a stone that fell to my stomach with a clank.

"It can't be Meera," Brigham said in a soft voice. "Her little brother seems very excited about getting a kitten today. We would know if they were already in his house. No six-year-old could ever keep that kind of secret." Aha! I'd thought they had realized it was me—but Andrew thought Meera was behind the account!

"It's Reuben, then," Andrew whispered. "I tell you, when I said I wanted a kitten, he blushed to the tips of his ears. You know—the way he does when he's nervous about making a shot? I know he's hiding something."

"Silence," the sub said. She was a young woman, older than my sister, way younger than my mom. She had a pinched face and long fake eyelashes, and she barely looked up from scrolling on her phone.

Andrew and Brigham kept whispering, but now I couldn't hear what they said.

"What do you think?" Solange asked softly, startling me. I hadn't realized she'd been looking at me the whole time.

"About what?"

She motioned with her head to the boys sitting a couple rows behind us. "Do you agree with them? That Reuben and Meera are behind the Kitten Cupid account?"

Sometimes in movies or books, the character says they

saw their whole life flash before their eyes when they experienced a near-death situation. Well, this time, the whole future flashed across my eyes. If Andrew didn't get what he wanted, a kitten, he would dig and dig until he found out who had passed him over, and then he'd destroy that person.

It was Slime Supreme all over again, except that this time, no one would be posting a recipe to keep people happy. Once the kittens were gone, they were gone.

Why had I thought an anonymous act would bring more happiness to our school? That gifting kittens would convince anyone to like me again? I was just ruining things even more.

Now I was in a mess, and I didn't know how to get out of it. But I had to keep these angry boys away from Meera and Reuben. Meera didn't know anything about the kittens, and Reuben had only been my helper. But if someone went to the principal with the wrong information, would she believe them? Would Reuben's reputation be ruined forever?

Maybe he'd seen this coming, and that's why he'd distanced himself from me. It had been so unfair of me to drag him into this mess.

Solange was waiting for my answer, so I shook my head and said, "No, I don't believe they have anything to do with it. Do you?"

Solange shrugged. "I'm not sure about Reuben. He's been talking about the kittens nonstop, and the way he talks about the gray one, Johnnycakes, it's like he knows him in real life. He's in love, and if he's not the Kitten Cupid, he should get that kitten."

My mouth went dry. Solange was right, and I needed to speak to Reuben to clear things up once and for all.

"Did you apply for one?" Solange asked, taking me by surprise.

"No," I said, and it wasn't even a lie. "And you?"

Solange smiled sadly. "I really wanted to, but my dad's allergic."

"That's too bad," I said, saying thanks in my heart that no one in my family was. "Can he take medicine for it?"

Solange laughed. "He tried, but after a while, the medicine stops having an effect on him. A long time ago, he and my mom said that if I really wanted a cat, I would have to volunteer at the shelter, so that's what I do every Saturday."

I looked at her like I'd never seen her before. "You do? I had no idea."

"It's the best of both worlds, actually," Solange said. "I get to play with the kittens and socialize them, but I don't have to do the hard stuff like cleaning up after them, you know? You do have to be sixteen or have an adult come with you, so my older brother volunteers too. My love for kittens spread over to him, and now he brings his girlfriend, who got her mom involved in fostering animals. It was like a chain of kitten love."

That was exactly what I had wanted to do as the Kitten Cupid. What if there was a way to continue the kitten love after my litter was placed with families?

"Isn't it hard that the kittens aren't yours to keep, though?" I asked.

Solange shook her head. "My maman told me once that

just because you love something or someone, that doesn't mean you have to own them, you know? It's like, I can love to look at a garden of flowers, but it doesn't mean I need to cut them and put them in vases in my house."

It all sounded very elegant when she said it in her accent. Her mom sounded like she'd get along with Mami and Beli.

"Maybe you could come with me, some day?" Solange asked, and it seemed like she'd been wanting to ask me for a long time but just didn't know how.

But in that moment, Lilah knocked on my classroom door and gave a yellow slip to the sub. The teacher read it and then looked up and said, "Natalia Flores? Principal Snow wants you in her office."

Chapter 15
Kindness Club

Last year I'd promised Mami that I'd never return to the principal's office, at least not for some drama that I had created. But here I was, sitting on the uncomfortable chair facing Mrs. Snow, and not because I was about to receive a ribbon for good behavior.

Reuben sat in the room next door, waiting for his turn. The school secretary, Mrs. Ali, tried to talk to him a couple of times, but he was quiet, looking out the window like the world was ending, even though the sun was shining. I couldn't believe I'd brought him into this mess with me.

"So, here we are, Natalia. *Again*," Mrs. Snow said, her elbows on the desk, and her hands clasped as if she were praying for patience. Her light brown eyes looked big behind her glasses, and I wondered what she saw when she looked at me.

"Here we are," I said, and then I bit my lip because I was sure I hadn't been supposed to answer.

Principal Snow sighed, and I held my breath.

Finally, she said, "I've been watching you for a long time."

I blushed to the tips of my ears, and the rush of blood to my head kind of hurt.

"I've seen how you struggled at the beginning of the year, and I'm sorry about that," she continued. "Last year you were one of my brightest students, but after the incident with the slime, and your dad's deployment, you turned into a little shadow. You've been so lonely."

I was surprised. I thought Mrs. Snow just thought I was a troublemaker.

"I had Reuben," I said, all too aware that I spoke in the past tense.

Mrs. Snow nodded. "You did, but then two things happened at once."

My heart was thumping. How did the principal see all of this happening? How did she know?

"After the break, you returned to class and you were still quiet, but the light was back in your eyes. At the same time, that cute Kitten Cupid AstroSnap account started getting all the likes from the students. Andromeda Elementary got kitten fever overnight. I feel the two events are linked. Am I right?"

I didn't know if I was supposed to keep an innocent face or own up to my crimes. I had to look away from her all-seeing eyes before she saw all the truth inside me—including the parts I wasn't proud of.

"How do you know about it?" I asked after a few seconds of heavy silence. There was no point in denying anything, but I wanted to know who had gone to the principal with the gossip.

"I know everything that happens in my school, young lady." Her voice wasn't loud, but I was sure that if it echoed inside me, the people outside the office could hear it too.

"I also noticed that at the same time the spark came back to your eyes, the whole school seemed . . . happier."

"Is that a bad thing?" I asked.

The corner of her mouth flickered. "Last year you promised you wouldn't use the school social media for any kind of secret ventures."

I hung my head in shame. I had promised. I couldn't deny that I'd broken my word.

"But also last year you said something that made me think. You said that slime had helped you to calm down when you were feeling anxious or sad, so you wanted other people to benefit from it too. Isn't that why you created Slime Supreme? To spread the joy? You told me you never did it for the money, even though you earned quite a bit from it."

She had heard me that day after all. Then why had she made me stop making my slime and sharing it with others?

"I didn't do it for the money," I agreed, unable to stay quiet any longer. "I only charged so I could afford more materials." Mrs. Snow arched an eyebrow, and I added softly, "I did what you said, and I closed the account. Also, when Meera posted the recipe, I didn't take it down."

"I know, and I also know how hard that must have been."

She had no idea.

Mrs. Snow gave a tiny smile. "I'll say this, although several people tried the recipe, they said it never turned out the same for them," the principal said, and I was tempted to ask if she was one of the people who'd tried it and couldn't figure it out.

"My grandma Beli says it's all in the hands," I said, and my voice sounded tiny, like Max's meows. I looked at my clenched fists on my lap. A small tub of slime or a purring kitten would be fantastic right now.

When I looked up at Mrs. Snow, she asked, "Tell me, what led you to create this elaborate operation to place the kittens?"

A little light seemed to come alive inside me. When I pictured the first time I found Gigi and her babies, the image took over me, until I felt the light spilling from my eyes. I felt like a real-life star emoji.

"The mom needed help, and I helped her. I can't keep all the babies, and I knew everyone at school would love them, so I thought that since not everyone would be able to adopt one, the rest of the people could at least enjoy the cuteness."

The principal looked at me with a strange expression in her eyes. "But you broke your word, and I remember your mom saying that if nothing else, you were honest. Creating a fake identity was not the honest way to do this."

Everyone had a FAstro, but saying so wouldn't fix this mess I'd created. And like she'd said before, she knew everything that happened in this school, and chances were, she was aware of all the FAstros in the system, including those like Andrew's, in which he showed his real face and character.

The principal continued, "Because this is the second time you've misused your account, I will have to revoke your privileges. Permanently."

At her words, a knot in my throat hurt more than when I'd been sick, and that was saying a lot. She wasn't done, though. "Last time we had an incident with a student misusing our social media, I ended up with a bitter taste in my mouth. So as part of the consequence for your actions, I'm going to go ahead and delete your Astro, and I'm also going to give you an assignment."

My shoulders sagged, and I was sure my face was falling too. What kind of assignment would I get? Wasn't deleting my Astro and being outcast from the school social life enough?

The principal stayed quiet, so I looked up at her, and she continued, "Your teacher Mrs. Thomas shared with me a paper you wrote for her a few weeks ago, about the need for our whole community to come together to protect animals. Why don't you send me an email with a project that will bring the school together in a more open way than the Kitten Cupid did? Does that sound fair to you?"

"A project to do what?" I asked, perplexed. Why couldn't she assign me something to do, sweeping the hallways, or sorting through the lost and found? I had no idea what she wanted.

She seemed to read my mind. Now she smiled widely and

said, "I'll only give you the project name: Kindness Club. Now you go and be creative with it."

If I rolled my eyes or groaned at her, I'd only get into even more trouble, so I just said, "Yes, ma'am."

I knew this wasn't going to end here. The principal would call my mom, and then I'd be paying for my actions until who knew when.

Thinking that Mrs. Snow was done with me, I stood up, and she said, "Now, ask Mr. Francis to come in. He also played a part in the project . . ."

My heart buckled. "No! Reuben had nothing to do with it."

"You're going to tell me he didn't help you plan anything? That he didn't know you were using your fake Astro to promote the kittens?"

Why did things sound so much worse when an adult like the principal spelled out each and every one of my mistakes?

Trying to calm my breathing, I said, "Reuben was just being a good friend."

He had been the best friend, and I couldn't drag him down with me.

The principal nodded once, but I wasn't sure it meant she believed me or not. "Very well," she said. "You're free to go back to your class. Ask Mr. Francis to step into my office so he can tell me his version of the events."

"Yes, ma'am," I replied.

When I walked out, Reuben looked up and his eyes were full of tears. I hadn't seen him cry since we were in first grade and he had fallen from the swings when I'd pushed him harder than he'd been expecting me to.

"Mrs. Snow wants to talk to you," I said. "Did you tell Meera about everything already?"

He looked as if I'd hit him. "Why would I do that?"

"You were spending a lot of time with her. I trusted you . . ."

He shook his head and said, "And I trusted that you'd notice I wanted a kitten all along, but you never even read my application."

I was so confused. "What are you talking about? You never applied!"

"Of course I did. The first day." In a flash, I remembered that deleted application. Was it his? Why didn't I go looking for it to check whose it was? Why had I been so thoughtless? Reuben was still speaking. "And I've been helping you since the first day, Natalia, but instead of noticing that I loved Johnnycakes, and that we're a perfect match, you were considering Brigham?"

"I never even considered Brigham for one second, Reuben. I just said that maybe loving a kitten was something his brother needed, and you took it the wrong way."

"The wrong way? I've wanted a kitten since I first saw them, and you always thought I was joking!"

"Why didn't you tell me clearly?" I asked, hyperaware that the principal and the office lady were witnessing our fight.

Reuben sighed and put his hands in his pockets. "I . . . was scared you'd say no. That I wouldn't be good enough for you."

And without another word, he turned around and walked into the principal's office.

Chapter 16
The Cat's Out
of the Bag

By the time I'd gone back to resource, it was only a few minutes until the final bell rang, but the whole school seemed to buzz with the latest scandal, once again featuring me in the center of it all.

"Natalia Flores is the Kitten Cupid!" Jojo said to Solange when she thought I couldn't hear.

Solange sent me a disappointed look. Not an hour ago I'd told her I wasn't involved. What would she think of me now?

Even the first graders knew the truth. The only person who seemed thrilled with the news was Bodhi, who ran up to me and said, "You had the kittens all this time? Oh, Nati! Can I come over and pet them?"

Meera walked in my direction and took her brother's hand. She seemed devastated, and I couldn't even look her in the eye. In a hurt hiss, she whispered, "Why did you let him get excited about getting a kitten? I know you'll never give him one, just because you're so mad at me."

Without giving me the chance to explain, she pulled Bodhi away to put him into their mom's SUV and stormed away to walk home herself.

Reuben stood beside the flagpole, looking at me and Meera with such sadness, I had to turn away and walk back home. I couldn't deal with his disappointment too.

I seethed all the way home, keeping as much distance from Meera as I could. When she reached the corner with the dogs, she hurried as she always did, but when I crested the hill, I saw she was waiting at the top for me.

"Was it really you?" she asked when I reached her, and her eyes were sparkling with tears. "I mean, the person I told all that personal stuff to on the application?"

"I'm not going to lie," I said. "Yes, it was me." All the anger I couldn't express for months wanted to erupt, but I didn't want to let all these emotions out. I was afraid of what I'd find if they came up to the surface.

Meera sighed and squared her shoulders. "I'm sorry about Slime Supreme, okay? I'm sorry I posted the secret recipe, Nati. I should've talked to you first. I shouldn't have worried so much about what the other kids wanted. But why would you lie all this time about the kittens?"

"I didn't lie."

"I trusted you," she said. "I felt like I knew the Kitten Cupid person, and it turns out I did. You must have never considered Bodhi, so why let him be so excited? I understand you're still mad at me, but why take it out on him?"

The high school bus stopped on the corner, and the two bulldogs started barking their heads off as the older kids got off the bus and walked home in the middle of the street. Before I could explain to Meera that I never expected things to get so complicated, she was caught up in the swarm of kids as she ran to her house. I didn't have a chance to tell her that I *was* considering Bodhi.

Mami wasn't back from the flower shop. I needed to talk

to her, but the day before Valentine's was their busiest day of the year, besides Mother's Day. She'd be gone until late.

I ran the last few feet to my house, opened the door, and called for Gigi. I longed for her purring to take the stress out of my heart. For her quiet company to tell me everything would be okay. Even if sometimes she gave me a side-eye because I woke up the kittens, I knew she loved me unconditionally.

"Gigi!" I called when she didn't come to greet me. I stood by the door, calling her name over and over, expecting to hear her velvety feet padding in my direction, and her gentle chirping that meant, *Hello, you're finally home.*

Gigi either didn't hear me or she too was mad at me for some reason. I dropped my backpack, with the note from the principal for my mom to sign, by the door and went straight to the laundry room. Maybe Mami or Julieta had come home for a minute and locked Gigi in with the babies to make sure the kittens didn't destroy the house.

But the laundry door was partially opened.

"Gigi?" I asked, peering inside.

Five little pairs of eyes looked up at me with fear. The kittens had been huddled in a mass of fur and love, and when they saw me, they meowed and rushed around me. Max arched her back just like Gigi did, and rubbed her head against my legs. Fifi and Harry sat quietly, just waiting for me to tell them where their mama was.

"Where's Gigi?" I asked softly, so they wouldn't get scared, and Meggie trilled like a little bird before she tucked herself in a corner. Johnnycakes opened his eyes for a second, and then he went back to sleep.

I stood frozen, not knowing what to do. If Gigi wasn't with her babies, where was she? Frantically, I looked all over the house, but there was no trace of my cat other than fur left behind on her favorite cushion by the window.

Gigi wasn't in any of her spots underneath the beds, on the windowsill, or on top of the shelf where Papi's photo looked down at me. I didn't want to panic, but my heart started racing, and my hands prickled with sweat.

Where could she be? She'd never leave her babies. She

was still so protective of them. Maybe someone had taken her from me. Someone who was mad that I'd been behind Kitten Cupid. With these thoughts buzzing in my mind, I looked everywhere again, hoping I'd find her asleep inside a box, or even the bathtub.

And then I saw it. The bathroom window that I'd left wide open in the morning. A cat could fit through that opening. Especially one as small as my Gigi.

Knowing there was no time to waste, I made sure the kittens were safe in the laundry room, and I ran out to look for Gigi. The first place I searched was the shed.

It seemed like a dream that I had found her here eight weeks ago, and that she'd chosen me to save her when she had no other friend. I'd helped her and fed her. I'd given her my whole heart, and now she had left me.

I looked inside the closet and the bins, but there were no traces of her.

I called out for her and rode my bike around the whole neighborhood time after time. My legs pumped harder and harder on the wet road, full of potholes after the winter snow. After one too many bumps, I slowed and climbed off my bike. I'd check one last time . . . as I walked home.

I hoped to find my bobtailed cat waiting for me around each corner, but she wasn't there.

When the vet had said that maybe Gigi had been separated from her family, I had judged them. I'd boasted that I could take the best care of her, and then I'd left the bathroom window open. Now she was gone. I'd only tried to spread happiness, and instead, I'd made a mess of everything. When I rescued Gigi and her babies, I'd only wanted them to be safe and happy. I thought I knew better than anyone who would love them the most. And I hadn't even been able to keep Gigi safe.

In a desperate move, I closed my eyes right there in the middle of the sidewalk and sent a prayer to the universe for forgiveness, and for help.

When I opened my eyes, my cat still wasn't there. Instead, a familiar car drove in my direction and slowed down until it stopped next to me.

"Nati?" Julieta asked, squinting as if she had a hard time seeing me in the semi-darkness of the street.

Before I could even start explaining, my shoulders started shaking. I put a hand over my mouth, but instead of hiding my crying, the hand made it sound like a snort-fart combination.

Under other circumstances, I'd have laughed, but now all I wanted was to stop the flood of emotions. My small hand couldn't contain them, and they came out in a wail that seemed to come from the bottom of my heart.

Chapter 17
Matching Game

After my sister helped me put my bike in the trunk (the front wheel stuck out, but our house was just a block away), I sat in the passenger seat, shivering with cold and fear.

"What's wrong?" said Julieta softly, leaving the car parked to turn to me. She placed a hand on my shoulder tentatively. How many times had I acted like a feral cat, avoiding all kinds of love and affection so I wouldn't hurt so much? I flinched at her touch, but my sister, my generous, kind sister, didn't move her hand away, and I finally melted into the moment and rested my head on her shoulder.

I let the tears flow, even when they ran off my nose in such an embarrassing way not all the sniffling in the world could contain them.

Julieta shushed me and caressed my hair, but didn't say anything. She only gave me the time and space I needed to cry—cry like I hadn't since Papi had left.

Finally, when the tears started to run out and the knot in my stomach didn't hurt so much anymore, I looked up.

My sister had the same look as the five kittens had the last time I saw them in the laundry room, gathered on their bed and staring at me as if asking where their mama was hiding. The sight of them had broken my heart, but now their need gave me something that had leaked out of me with the tears. A motivation.

They still needed me to get them their perfect homes.

I'd planned on them going to their forever homes tonight, and I didn't want any of them to leave without saying good-bye to Gigi. But everyone would be waiting. My heart swelled with love for my fluffballs. It still hurt that Gigi was gone, but the babies needed me, and if I really loved them, I'd do what was best for them.

And of course I did really love them—all of them equally. Like Julieta and Beli had told me, love isn't a pie. I didn't have to divide my love up between them—I would always have more than enough to go around.

Finally, I took a shuddering breath and said it aloud. "Gigi's lost."

The words sank in the silence that followed and made my ears ring.

"Oh, Nati Natasha," Juli said.

"I left the bathroom window open, and—"

"And she ran away," Julieta said.

"I only wanted to make people happy, but I made everything worse!"

Julieta looked skeptical. "You made things worse? How?"

"The principal deactivated my Astro access. My friends are mad at me, along with everyone else," I said, ticking off the reasons with my fingers. "Reuben's hurt that I never saw the application he sent because I deleted it by accident and didn't realize until today. I never thought he was serious when he kept saying he wanted Johnny for himself." I dried my eyes with the inside of my shirt and continued. "Meera is hurt that I never told her. And the entire school knows that

I was behind the whole Kitten Cupid thing, and now no one will want one, and Mami will know I failed. I couldn't spread happiness like I told her I would. I couldn't change people's minds about last year. The shelter will be full now that it's almost kitten season. Who'll want the kittens?"

Julieta kept caressing my hair and said, "Hayden will be heartbroken if he can't have Fifi, but he'll understand if you think another home is better for her."

There was no better match for Fifi than Hayden. I'd always known that.

"You still have the printed-out applications, right?" Julieta asked. "Why don't you contact the people and see what they have to say before you jump to conclusions? If they say yes, then I'll drive you around to deliver the bundles of joy. If not, we'll figure something out."

"But Gigi won't get to say goodbye to them," I said.

Julieta looked ahead at the dark road. "Let's drive around the neighborhood one more time. I mean, what can we lose, right?"

I hugged her tightly and said, "You're my favorite sister."

"I'm your only sister!" She laughed softly and turned the engine on.

Julieta drove in silence along the same streets I'd scoured with my bike. Every time we hit a pothole, the trunk lid bounced against the wheel. I bit my lip, straining my eyes to see in the darkened streets, hoping to catch a glimpse of white velvety paws, or the flash of blinking yellow eyes. I rolled down the window, but all I heard were the barks of the neighborhood dogs.

Julieta sighed. I knew she didn't want to say we wouldn't find Gigi. For all I knew, my cat had never been so far from our house, but maybe she'd try to go to her first human's home. Julieta turned on Reuben's street, and she screeched to a stop.

The sidewalks were covered in ice, but there, in the middle of the street, a person walked briskly, holding something in their arms. Julieta drove to the curb, and when I looked out the window to see better, I thought I recognized the way the person walked. His hair was sticking out in all directions, but he carried that bundle as if he had a treasure.

"Gigi!" I called, and a tiny meow answered.

"Are you kitten me!" Reuben's voice exclaimed when the cat he'd been holding wiggled in his arms, wanting to get free, until she finally dropped to the ground.

"No!" Julieta, Reuben, and I cried as Gigi looked around, disoriented, as if she didn't know where to dart and hide.

Without another thought, I got out of the car and called again, in the softest voice I could manage. "Gigi, girl. I'm here, sweetheart."

Gigi must have heard the desperation in my voice, or maybe she was just worried about how sad I sounded.

She meowed, as if saying, *There you are!* and darted toward me. I knelt down to catch her in my arms, and I hugged her.

"Oh, my queen, I missed you," I said, tears falling freely.

Gigi sniffed my face, and then her dainty tongue licked my tears, always a mama taking care of her loved ones. She had grown so much since I saw her the first time. Even in the semi-darkness, her coat looked shiny and long. Her tail was still a stump, but she twitched her ears to let me know she too was happy we were together again.

Finally, she looked at me with a question on her beautiful face.

"They're waiting for a last see-you-later kiss," I said.

Reuben stood on the sidewalk watching Gigi and me. I had so many questions, but all I could say was "Thank you."

He walked toward me, and even though Julieta was watching from the car, I wrapped an arm around his shoulder and pressed him tight in a hug. Gigi meowed to warn me not to squish her, and we laughed.

"She came to my house," Reuben said, speaking fast. "When I heard the meows, I couldn't believe it was really her. I tried to call you, but no one answered the phone, so I was bringing her home."

My heart thumped hard in my chest as I said, "Reuben, thanks for being such a good friend. Especially because I haven't been such a great friend back. I never should have made you choose between me and Meera."

His eyes widened. "I know why you were upset last year.

But I know why Meera was too. I just wish the two of you would talk to each other so I won't have to lie to anyone."

"I'm sorry I asked you to do that." I hung my head but made sure to meet his amber eyes. Under the moonlight, they looked a little like a cat's, more specifically like Johnnycakes's, Reuben's perfect match. "Come to the house with us," I offered. "Your Johnnycakes is waiting for you."

Reuben placed a hand over his heart as he stepped back to better look at us. "*My* Johnnycakes? But . . . the application was lost."

Even Julieta laughed from the car. Gigi flattened her ears at the loud sound.

"Reuben, the only thing I need to know is that your parents are okay with it. I already know you'll always protect Johnny."

"Woo-hoo!" Reuben exclaimed. "What are we waiting for, then?"

We got back in the car, my cat nestled next to my heart, my sister humming a song, and my friend smiling in the back.

Chapter 18
Homecoming and Going

The goodbye kisses were too sweet not to get teary-eyed. As soon as Gigi took a look at her kids, she ran to them, and one by one, gave them a last bath. The kittens usually wrestled each other nonstop, swung from the curtains and the tablecloths, and waited by the laundry room to attack the ankles of anyone who dared walk between the kitchen and the bathroom (that is, everyone). But this time, they waited patiently for their own turn for a last moment with their mama. Now it was Fifi's turn. Fifi, who never came first with anyone. Maybe Gigi had known that among the babies Fifi had been the one who'd received less affection and was now trying to send her off with the best memories.

Who knew what secrets were hidden underneath Gigi's

purrs? What advice was she telling her kids? I hoped that they knew that if they got lost, they could always come home.

A few days ago, I had prepared a box for each of the babies. The box contained a blanket with their mama's scent, a birth certificate, a stuffed animal to hug, their records of their weight, a copy of their adoption contract with the vet's info for vaccines and the spay-or-neuter appointment, and the sweaters Beli had knitted for them. We threw in cutout paper hearts and a kitty-themed Valentine's Day card with our congratulations.

While Gigi and her babies had their last moment together, Julieta let me use her phone to text the chosen families. Reuben helped me check that the kittens' going-away boxes were ready, but my heart drummed anxiously as I waited for the replies to come. I jumped every time the phone pinged with an incoming text.

One by one, the four replies arrived. Each family was more excited than the next. None of them turned their kitten down. None of them turned *me* down.

Finally, Julieta looked at the clock and asked, "Should we go?"

We placed the boxes in the car and headed out. Reuben sat in the back to make sure the kittens didn't climb out of their carriers, but by the silence, I could tell everyone was behaving. Maybe they were surprised by the new experience of a car ride.

I rang the bell at the first stop, and Jojo and Sam opened their apartment door, grinning as I exclaimed, "Happy Valentine's Day!" Jojo's cheeks were bright pink and her blue eyes sparkled with excitement as her mom peered into the box and smiled at the sight of the kitten.

"Thank you," Jojo said, hugging Harry to her chest. Sam smiled at me, and I was so happy seeing the joy the kitten had brought their family that I didn't even have time to be teary-eyed. Soon, after a few instructions, it was time for the second delivery.

Hayden was next, and he was waiting with the door wide open.

He ran to meet us at the curb, and he was so excited that

he grabbed the box from Julieta's hands and ran back into his house to introduce Fifi to his parents without kissing Julieta.

"See you later," we called, and he waved us goodbye.

"Thank you, Nati," Julieta said as we headed off to the next stop. "I'll never be able to top this Valentine's Day gift."

Reuben sat in the back with two kittens nestled on his lap. The next stop was easy because I knew it was such a perfect match. As we pulled up in front of a big house, a commercial played on the TV, and the smell of cookies curled from underneath the door. The perfect home for Meggie to grow up into the sunshine kitten she was becoming.

When I was about to knock, Lilah opened the door.

Her green eyes went wide with excitement. I offered the box with Meggie inside to her, and when she saw her alert little face peeking out, Lilah's tears started flowing. "For real?"

I couldn't really speak, so I nodded as the box passed from my hands to hers.

I watched as she carefully placed it on the floor. Before

she lifted the blanket, I stepped into the house and closed the door. One escaped kitten was enough to last me a lifetime.

Lilah gasped. "She's gorgeous! More beautiful in person than in pictures and videos!"

Carefully, she scooped up Meggie from the tiny nest. Meggie immediately bumped her little head against Lilah's nose.

"That means she loves you already," I said.

Lilah was speechless. Maybe sensing something special was happening, her mom peered into the room and smiled at me. "Thank you," she said. "With Lilah's older siblings moved out, our family was ready for a tiny furry creature to love. Lilah's always wanted a kitten, and now our family's complete."

I went back to the car with empty arms, but a full heart. The stars were bright and popping out of the velvet sky.

My queen Georgiana, my kitten finally, was waiting for me in the front seat. Her huge yellow eyes reflected the stars, and when she blinked, I knew she meant *thank you* for finding the perfect homes for her babies.

We still had one more stop, though.

"Bodhi?" Julieta asked.

I nodded, and looking back at Reuben, I said, "And Meera."

"Meow, meow!" Reuben exclaimed, and kissed Johnny on the head.

I wished Reuben would say one of his jokes to make me laugh, but the next stop was Max's future family. I'd wanted to keep her for myself, this kitten I had fed with so much love for so many weeks. This kitten that had been at the brink of passing on to cat heaven, but who'd fought so hard for her life. And although it hurt to see her go, the family she was going to was the perfect match for my rainbow kitten.

Julieta stopped the car, and as I got out with Max in her box, I took a deep breath. The night was clear and pure, and the cold air blew all my doubts away. This was what I needed to do.

Reuben and I walked up to the front door.

The Rogerses' home had a pink light in every window and dozens of construction paper hearts pasted on the door. Meera opened it to us with the same wonder in her eyes that had welcomed us in every one of the homes I'd chosen for the kittens. We looked at each other and Meera nodded slightly.

"He's playing with his stuffed kittens in his room," she said, guiding me in.

We followed her up a flight of stairs, and I opened the door to Bodhi's room.

He played under a gauze canopy, cat-ear headband on his head, reading to his stuffed kittens. When he heard me enter, he turned around to look over his shoulder. His eyes filled with tears when he saw the box in my hands.

"Niño Gato," I said, "are you ready to become a kitten protector?"

There was no joy like the light on Bodhi's face. He and little Max went together like cheese and dulce de guava. Carefully, he took Max out of the box, and she nestled against the crook of Bodhi's neck as if she'd done it a million times before. I'd been feeling so sad about giving Max away, but Bodhi would clearly do absolutely anything for her. Bodhi whispered in her ears, and I caught a few of his words. "I know Nati named you Max, but I think you're an arco iris, a rainbow. What do you think, *Iris*?"

Meera looked at me alarmed, like she was afraid I'd complain he was already changing the kitten's name. But love means sometimes you need to let go, and I loved this kitten and Bodhi.

As he began introducing the kitten to each stuffed animal in the room, Meera and I walked out of the room. Reuben stayed with Bodhi, showing him how Max—Iris— liked to chase strings around the room.

"We have a kitten station in the mudroom," Meera said. "I hope it's okay."

She sounded so nervous, like we'd never been best friends before.

Love means letting go.

Letting go of kittens, of sisters going to college to start

the next chapter, and of grudges that hurt so much in the past but that I'd made worse for not wanting to forgive. This wasn't the way to spread kindness and love.

"Meera," I said, "can you forgive me for never trying to understand your side of the story with Slime Supreme? Reuben didn't want to choose between you and me because he said he could understand how both of us felt. I wish—" My voice broke. I'd missed her so much.

Meera chewed a fingernail. "I wish I had asked you before posting the recipe. I didn't know how to make everyone happy when they couldn't get into the lottery, but I also didn't realize how special that recipe was to you. I thought of everyone else's feelings but yours, and I lost you. I'm sorry. I missed you so much, Nati." I reached out my arms, and she hugged me back hard.

"Oh, my whiskers!" Reuben exclaimed from behind, making Meera and me jump. "I'm purr-plexed! But don't get me wrong, it's cat-tastic that you guys are friends again!" He hugged both Meera and me.

"I'm sorry," I said to both of them. "No more grudges."

Meera flicked her hair to the side and said, "No more secrets, okay? Especially when it's about kittens."

We laughed, but I actually had a favor to ask her, and while Bodhi introduced Max—Iris—to the whole family, I told Meera and Reuben about Mrs. Snow's Kindness Club assignment. I wanted her and Reuben to be the first ones in on the plan.

Chapter 19
Cupid's Arrows

After we said goodbye to Meera and her family, Julieta and I dropped off Reuben and Johnnycakes at home. His mom fell in love with the kitten as soon as she laid eyes on him. Johnny would never lack for love and attention.

Back home, after I sent an email to Mrs. Snow, we settled in to watch a movie, Juli, my Gigi, and I. Soon, a car rumbled to a stop in the carport.

But when I turned to see if it was Hayden coming over with cookies, I saw Mami standing at the door.

She smiled and said, "I missed my little cupid girl."

And without missing a beat, she came up to me and hugged me.

A sigh escaped my lips. I melted into Mami's arms. I'd

missed being nestled against her, in that scent of her hair that meant home.

Gigi sat daintily in between us, purring, healing my heart and telling me everything would be all right.

"You kept my favorite," Mami said.

"It was the only choice. It's all her fault after all, so she's stuck with us."

Mami laughed, and it was the most beautiful sound in the world.

"You're early," I said.

She smiled her Cheshire-cat smile that said so much without words. "We have a lot to catch up on, young lady. I just got a message from Mrs. Snow." I winced as I held my breath. "She told me about your fake account and the complicated plan for the kittens." Mami looked stern. "We'll talk about it. But she also loved the proposal for the Kindness Club you sent her tonight. She said that the whole school will love the idea of holding a class-wide volunteer day at the Andromeda shelter for Kindness Club. It's brilliant, and I'm proud of you."

My breath rushed out of me. "Well," I said carefully, "kitten season is almost here, so we need all the foster families we can get."

Mami pressed her lips but then started laughing. "Ay, ay, ay! What did we get ourselves into?" But her eyes were sparkling, so I knew that in spite of her words, she would be able to forgive me.

"At least now we know what to do with newborn kittens. Sending them off to their families and saying goodbye won't be as hard anymore," Julieta said.

I suspected saying goodbye would always be hard. I didn't even want to think of the moment my sister left for college in the fall, but in the last eight weeks, I'd learned that spreading kindness and happiness meant letting go. That love didn't fade with time and distance or get divided between people.

"Beli said she'd do her own version of the Kindness Club with Tío Mako and the girls at the local shelter in Puerto Rico," Mami added. "Nati, who would've thought one little act of kindness on a stormy night could affect people and animals all the way across the continent and the ocean?"

"Meow, meow!" I exclaimed, because although I was getting better at rolling my *r*'s, I still didn't know how to purr, and the happiness spilling over my heart could only be expressed in cat-isms.

The news was too meowgical to keep to ourselves.

"We need to tell Papi," I said. "Is it too late to call him?"

Mami and Julieta exchanged one of those looks of surprise, but only for a second.

My mom looked at her watch and said, "It's already after eight a.m. there. I'm sure he's around."

My heart pounded so hard as she dialed the number and then the phone rang. Gigi slept on my lap, and before my nerves got the best of me, she started purring again as if she knew I needed all the support I could get.

And then he answered, and I saw his smiley, tanned face on the tiny phone screen.

"Happy San Valentín, Papi," I said. It was already February 14 where he was.

"Feliz San Valentín, beba," he exclaimed.

And I told him the truth.

It was all the cat's fault. It was her fault that my heart didn't feel like a stone anymore, that I'd learned to forgive and let my heart heal. It was her fault I learned that a mom can't love one baby more than the other. Sometimes, one just needs a little more attention.

It was her fault that I'd found a project that could spread happiness and kindness to the whole town and beyond. It was all Gigi's fault. And the little queen knew it.

Acknowledgments

Writing this book brought such joy into my life, and it wouldn't have been possible without the support, trust, guidance, and inspiration I received from my meowgical editor Olivia Valcarce. Gracias, gracias, gracias! The title is purrfect!

Thanks to my agent, Linda Camacho, and the Gallt & Zacker family. How did I get so lucky to be on your team?

All my gratitude and appreciation to editor extraordinaire Aimee Friedman, as well as Jana Haussmann, Caroline Flanagan, Jackie Hornberger, Priscilla Eakeley, Claire Flanagan, Jessica Rozler, Jennifer Rinaldi, Jordana Kulak, Julia Eisler, and everyone else at Scholastic who helps get this book into kids' hands. And to the Scholastic Book Fairs and Book Clubs teams for championing stories.

Thank you to my writing communities: SCBWI, VCFA, The Harried Plotters, Madcap Retreats, Pitchwars, Write Out Camp, Storymakers, and WYFIR. To Las Musas

Collective, the Latinx Kidlit and IBPOC communities, and Latinos in Action, gracias, familia!

Diane Telgen, thank you for all your expertise and, most importantly, your friendship. Te quiero!

Thank you, Jen Cervantes, my friend and beta reader.

Veeda Bybee, dearest friend, thanks for listening to me, checking up on me, and being my accountability partner for #5amwritersclub even though we're now in different time zones. I treasure our friendship.

Verónica Muñoz and Rachel Seegmiller, nothing would be possible without you. Thank you!

Mis amigas queridas: Aída, Karina, Anedia, Paty, Hilda Price, Alicia Hortal Campbell, Tania, Iris, and Juli, gracias totales!

Gracias a mis hermanos por siempre creer en mí, especialment Damián por las noches sin dormir cuando éramos chiquitos y teníamos una mascota que cuidar (RIP, Daisy).

Thanks to all my family, especially Jeff, Juli, Maga, Joax, Lel, and Valen, for all your support and, more than anything, the inspiration to come up with adventures for my characters! Thanks also to the cat angels in my life who inspired Queen Georgiana: Mamushka, Gigi, and her meowjesty Queen Coraline.

Last but not least, thank you to my wonderful readers! You make it all possible. Meow, meow!

Ways to Help

There are many organizations devoted to helping animals that depend on volunteers for all they do. While writing this story, I turned to my friend, writer and editor Diane Telgen, for advice on how to support these organizations. She has volunteered and fostered cats and kittens with various groups in three states over more than fifteen years, and graciously answered so many questions, not only about cats, but also about shelters. Any mistakes in this book are my own. Here are some of the different types of rescues that Diane said may need your support:

• Animal Care & Control (AC&C): These city departments deal with strays, cruelty cases, and hoarding cases found by animal-control officers, as well as animals relinquished by the public. These groups serve on the front lines; despite the best efforts of staff and volunteers, these frequently overburdened shelters may have to euthanize for space.

- <u>City-Affiliated Humane Societies:</u> These organizations are not part of the local government, but have a contract with the city to take in strays and investigate cruelty cases. With large volunteer and foster programs, these facilities can have very high save rates.

- <u>Large Private Shelters:</u> These self-funded groups don't have government contracts, but rehome animals taken from city AC&Cs and members of the public. They have large facilities and the support of robust fundraising programs and large volunteer and foster networks. They get to choose their animals, so they rarely euthanize unless it's for medical or behavioral reasons.

- <u>Small Independent Rescues:</u> These are run by a few individuals. They may have a small facility, or they may use a big foster network instead. Some specialize in a particular breed of cat or dog, or animals with special needs, or just cats/just dogs. Many will house animals until they are rehomed.

Although most animal shelters have volunteer programs, state laws mean there can be age restrictions. Some groups restrict kids to administrative tasks, or only allow contact with animals if accompanied by a parent. But some have special training programs for teen volunteers, and most allow families with kids to become fosters. Check with your local shelter or Humane Society chapter to find out how you can help!

Visit your local chapters of The Humane Society (humanesociety.org), The Kitten Lady (kittenlady.org), and Alley Cat Allies (alleycat.org), among others, for wonderful information and instructional videos on kitten care and cat rescue.

Find more reads you will love . . .

Vanesa Campos can't wait for winter vacation. Her week at Pinecloud Lodge promises skiing, hot cocoa, and maybe even some new friends. But suddenly, Vanesa's little brother, Hunter, is stranded out in the blizzard! Vanesa will have to team up with snooty Beck and twins Emma and Eric—plus one giant dog—to rescue him. Can she save her brother and discover which real friends will weather the storm with her?

When a girl and her dog play cupid, there's sure to be a mess...

the love pug

j.j. howard
Author of *Pugs and Kisses*

SCHOLASTIC

wish

Emma's pug, Cupid, has a hidden talent: He is a master at matchmaking! Her pet seems to have a nose for spotting which two people belong together. But as Emma tries to navigate crushes and secrets, she finds that things are a lot more complicated than they seem. And what if Cupid also has a surprising match in mind . . . for Emma herself?